The Boyfriend

Joanna leaned over and, her hand trembling, struggled to turn on the bed-table lamp ... just as Dex pulled himself into the room.

He grinned at her, that warm, familiar grin, and walked stiffly away from the window into the yellow light.

"Hi, Joanna." His voice was a whisper, almost ghostly.

"Dex?"

"Yeah. It's me."

Don't scream, don't scream, don't scream...

"But – Dex – you're dead!"

Classic Point Horror ... it's better than ever!

Look out for:

April Fools
Trick or Treat
Richie Tankersley Cusick

Happy Valentine's Day ... not...

Dream Date
Sinclair Smith

The Boyfriend
The Dead Girlfriend
The Girlfriend
R. L. Stine

Point Horror

The Boyfriend

R. L. STINE

■ SCHOLASTIC

Scholastic Children's Books,
Commonwealth House, 1-19 New Oxford Street,
London WC1A 1NU, UK
a division of Scholastic Ltd
London ~ New York ~ Toronto ~ Sydney ~ Auckland
Mexico City ~ New Delhi ~ Hong Kong

First published in the US by Scholastic Inc, 1990
First published in the UK by Scholastic Ltd, 1992
This edition published by Scholastic Ltd, 1999

ISBN 0 590 11368 2

Printed by Cox and Wyman Ltd, Reading, Berks.

10 9 8 7 6 5 4 3 2

The Boyfriend

Chapter 1

Am I going to do it? Joanna asked herself.

She looked down the brightly lit mall at the blur of faces, shoppers balancing packages, pulling young children, peering into colorful display windows, teenagers walking in twos and threes, beginning their Friday night prowl.

Of course I am, Joanna decided, a smile spreading slowly across her face. Once I get something in my mind, I always go through with it.

"Daddy's little go-getter." That's what Sherman Collier, Joanna's father, always called her. His highest compliment: "Daddy's little go-getter. She'll never take no for an answer."

There were lots of compliments from Dad, Joanna thought bitterly, walking quickly away from the meeting place by the bookstore, crossing the wide aisleway, then stopping. I was Daddy's girl, "a *real* Collier."

Of course, thought Joanna, her smile now completely gone, that didn't stop him from leaving. That didn't stop him from running off with that cheap-looking redhead, off to Tucson or some crazy place. Her mother refused to tell her where.

She hadn't heard from her father since, not even on her sixteenth birthday.

Mom had done all right, though, thought Joanna. Tiny, meek little Mom. Well, she wasn't so meek when divorce time came around. She must have taken Daddy for every penny he had, which was considerable. The two of them had lived really well ever since. Mom and Joanna. They enjoyed being rich and not having Daddy around.

At least Joanna did.

Daddy's little go-getter didn't miss Daddy at all.

So why was she standing on the edge of this mall now, watching the Friday night crowd pour in, thinking about him?

Breakups.

That was why.

Family breakups. Boyfriend breakups.

Breakups weren't so sad. In fact, they could lead to better things.

She thought of Shep. His wavy blond hair. The dimple in his left cheek when he smiled that funny, lopsided smile. She wondered what Shep was doing tonight while she was supposed to be meeting Dex.

What was that song on the loudspeaker? Some ancient Elvis song from the fifties. "Don't Be Cruel."

Joanna nearly laughed out loud. Don't be cruel? Why not?

It was a cruel world.

She was about to do something really cruel. And, she had to admit, she was enjoying it already.

She turned and caught her reflection in the candle store window. Not bad, she thought.

She knew she was beautiful. Why should she force herself to have false modesty and pretend she didn't know, like some simpering young thing in one of those embarrassing Elvis movies Dex had forced her to watch on TV?

She had the Collier good looks. That's what her father always told her — usually as a dig at her mother. She had the high cheekbones, the perfect, straight nose, the clear blue eyes that always seemed to be opened wide, the proud, high forehead, and the sunlight-blonde hair, so smooth and straight that it looked beautiful even cut so stylishly short.

The Collier good looks.

Maybe that's why she and her mother could never be that close, as close as other girls and their mothers. Or was that something from a dumb fifties movie, too?

Her mousy little mother. She always looked so small and funny inside the glamorous fur coat she wore everywhere with the collar pulled up almost over her head. It always made Joanna laugh — to herself, of course.

She couldn't blame her father for wanting a little more.

Yes she could.

Breakups.

Well, of course breakups were on her mind tonight.

Two wiry twelve-year-old boys on skateboards came whirring down the aisle. One of them nearly barreled into her. Joanna jumped out of the way just in time. "Hey, you — " She stopped herself.

The mall police would catch them sooner or later.

And she didn't want to call attention to herself. She was hiding, after all. Hiding from Dex.

Hiding from her boyfriend.

She thought of how Dex smelled. Sort of fresh. Almost flowery. Soapy.

It almost made her sad.

Almost.

Was that him across the hall at their usual meeting place?

No. It was some other guy in jeans and a rock T-shirt.

She leaned against the concrete column, the back of her head resting against a sign announcing some kind of mall band concert.

What kind of jerks would go out of their way to listen to a band playing in a mall? It was no wonder people turned their noses up at the suburbs. Everything here in Middlewood was so . . . tacky. Joanna knew she would move to New York as soon as she graduated. Enroll in a few modeling programs. And with her fabulous looks and drive, well . . . who knew how far she could go?

Which was one reason why Dex had to go.

There he was now. Hurrying to the bookstore entrance where they always met. Late again.

He'll be late his whole life, she thought, surprised by her bitterness. He'll never catch up.

He stopped in front of the open entranceway, looking from side to side. He seemed to relax. From across the crowded aisle, she could see that he looked relieved.

He thinks I'm late, too. What a hoot.

Look at him, she thought disapprovingly, pressing herself flat against the column so he couldn't see her. That's how he dresses for a date. Those faded jeans, torn at the knee. That stupid T-shirt. Probably not even a clean one.

He did have that wonderful, soapy smell, though. And when they were all alone late at night in the front seat of her car, he . . . Well, why get into that?

She was standing him up, after all.

And watching him while she did it.

She shifted her down vest to her other hand. Across the wide aisle, Dex started to pace back and forth in front of the bookstore. He looked at his watch. He jammed his hands into his jeans pockets and continued to pace.

He's short, she thought. Why hadn't she ever noticed how short he was? And his jeans are baggy in back.

Look how nervous he's getting. He knows I'm never late.

And he knows I've been losing interest in him.

I haven't been too subtle about that, have I!

You're cruel, Joanna, she told herself. Actually, it's one of your most admirable qualities.

How else to survive in a cruel world?

Dex would have to find it out sooner or later.

Why not sooner? This was good for him.

He stopped pacing. He ran his hand back nervously through his thick, black hair.

She had loved to pull on Dex's hair, tug at the back, tease him, pulling until it hurt. Now it just looked greasy to her.

Get a haircut, she thought.

No. Don't go overboard, Joanna. You love his hair. Don't deny it. You love the way it tickles your cheek when he puts his head on your shoulder and pulls you close.

I'm not giving in, she thought, shifting her weight against the column. She straightened her blue sweater, the one her father had bought because it matched her eyes so perfectly. It was getting a bit tight now. Why did she insist on wearing it?

I'm not running over to him. I'm just going to stand here and watch him squirm. I'm enjoying this too much.

He looked angry now. He stopped pacing and stood with his hands in his pockets, looking down the aisle toward the movie theater at the end.

"Breaking Up Is Hard To Do," Joanna thought. What was that? An old song title? Well, she knew it wasn't going to be easy with Dex. He was so dramatic, so moody, so theatrical.

Dex wanted to be an actor. And he had the dark good looks for it. He looked a lot like the actor Matt Dillon. Sounded like him, too.

The previous spring, he had invited Joanna to come see him in the lead role in *Julius Caesar* at his school across town. Joanna obligingly came, worrying if her BMW would be safe parked on the street across from the three-story brick school. The neighborhood didn't look very appealing. She had locked the car and hurried into the building, surprised by how tacky and run-down everything looked. It had been so long since Joanna had been inside a public school.

Dex had been good. He had a clear, expressive voice, and he looked very handsome on the stage. But everyone else was terrible, the scenery was practically nonexistent, and the lights kept flickering.

Afterwards, Dex was so excited. He was positively high! Joanna told him how good he was. But all the while she was feeling sorry for him. If only his aunt could afford to send him to a private school, like Landover, where Joanna went. Then maybe he'd have a chance to get somewhere with his acting ambitions.

But his old aunt had no money at all. And she hadn't wanted to become Dex's guardian in the first place. She didn't care if he went to school or not. She lived in her own gray world.

A world I don't ever want to be pulled into, Joanna thought, watching Dex across the mall. Two guys she had never seen before had stopped to talk to him. She could hear them laughing about something, but Dex didn't join in, and he kept looking past them, looking for her.

This anxiety will help Dex's acting career, Joanna thought. Heartbreak. An actor needs some heartbreak in his life to draw on during his performances, right?

"Heartbreak Hotel." Wasn't that an Elvis song, too?

Why do I have Elvis on the brain? she wondered. I guess Dex looks a little like the young Elvis, the Elvis in all those movies. Was that why Dex liked watching those old films so much?

Time to go home, she decided suddenly.

The two guys had headed on to the movie theater. Dex was alone again, pacing back and forth in front of the bookstore entrance.

This is so mean, she thought, turning her back on him and heading to the doors that led to the parking lot.

So why do I feel like laughing?

Chapter 2

"So you just stood there and watched him?"

Mary's voice rose several octaves as she asked the question. Joanna pulled the phone away from her ear before the high-pitched voice did any damage. She could just picture Mary, lying on her stomach on her bed, a shocked look on her angelic little face.

"Yeah. It was kind of . . . interesting," Joanna said. She knew that would get a reaction from her friend — and it did.

"Interesting? Joanna — that's so cold!" Mary cried.

Mary was always so sweet, so nice to everyone. So angelic. Joanna loved shocking her, making her voice rise.

Across town, Mary, lying on her stomach on the bed, in the oversized man's shirt she used for a nightshirt, looked at the phone as if to ask, "Am I really hearing right?" Her brown hair, falling in tight curls down her neck and shoulders, was still wet from the shower. She shivered.

But she knew that it was Joanna who was making her feel cold.

How can this person be my friend? The question flashed through her mind. And then: Why has Joanna changed so much?

They had been friends since grade school. When Mary's family moved out of Middlewood to the less fashionable area known as Westside, the friendship had continued, mostly over the phone.

Joanna had always been a little snobbish, Mary realized. And that snooty private school she went to had done a lot to make her even more so. But she was so smart and funny, and so pretty, and such a good friend, someone you could always talk to, confide in, tell just about everything.

So when had she turned so cold, so mean?

Had she been that way all along, and Mary simply hadn't noticed?

No, Mary thought, as Joanna's voice continued to murmur in her ear. No. Joanna has changed. Since the divorce, I guess. . . .

"You'll have to meet Shep," Joanna was saying. "I think you'll really like him. He's very good-looking, and — "

"He goes to Landover?" Mary asked.

"Yeah. He's a senior this year. He's already been accepted at Yale. Everyone in his family goes to Yale."

"Nice," Mary said. She didn't really know what to say. "I — I'm just so surprised. I mean, totally.

I thought you and Dex were really serious."

"We were," Joanna said. "Too serious. It wasn't good for either of us."

"What do you mean, Joanna?"

"I mean Dex has no money and never will have," Joanna replied, talking very quickly, the way she always did when she got excited. "Sure, I care about him. But a person has to be practical, too."

"Practical?" Mary truly was shocked, more by Joanna's voice than anything else. She sounded so hard, so removed, as if she were talking about a stranger.

"I'm thinking of both of us," Joanna said, not meaning to sound as defensive as she did. "I mean, how do you think Dex feels being driven around in my BMW all the time?"

"I don't think it bothers him," Mary said drily. Then she added, "You know, Dex wouldn't mind taking the bus once in a while."

Joanna laughed. "Get real. I'm really going to take the bus with a $40,000 BMW sitting in the garage!"

This isn't the first time she's told me how much her car cost, Mary thought, brushing back her wet hair uncomfortably. "What kind of car does Shep drive?" she asked, unable to keep the sarcasm from her voice.

"He has one of those cute Cabriolet convertibles," Joanna said. "A red one with a white top."

Which did she check out first — Shep or his car? Mary wondered. Then she scolded herself for starting to sound as cold as Joanna. This is just an act Joanna is putting on, Mary thought. She doesn't want to let on to me how bad she feels about breaking up with Dex. She probably doesn't even want to admit it to herself. So she's putting on this cruel act, pretending to be tough.

"Are you sure you know what you're doing?" Mary asked her old friend. "Dex is crazy about you."

"He's just plain crazy," Joanna said, sighing. "Know what he's been doing lately? He takes the crosstown bus over here in the middle of the night and climbs in my bedroom window. Just to talk."

"Sounds very romantic," Mary said, trying not to sound jealous.

"Are you kidding?! If my mother ever found out, she'd — she'd ground me for a month!"

And that $40,000 BMW would just sit in the garage, Mary thought.

"Dex is too melodramatic," Joanna continued. "He's too theatrical for me. He's — " There was a series of clicks on the line. "Hold on, Mary — I've got another call coming in."

The phone went silent on Mary's end. Frowning, she sat up. She placed the receiver down on the bedspread and went to get a bath towel to dry her hair.

"Hello?" Joanna asked brightly. She had a good idea who was calling. "Oh, hi, Dex." Keep it casual, she told herself.

"Hey — I'm still at the mall," he said. He sounded very upset. She could just picture the look on his face, his dark eyebrows low over his eyes.

He was probably biting the skin off his lower lip the way he always did.

"What? *Where* are you?" That's good. That sounds really innocent.

"I thought we had a date, Joanna. You were supposed to meet me — remember?"

"Huh?" She laughed. She knew the laugh would really infuriate him. "Oh, good lord! I completely forgot!"

Silence on his end.

More silence.

A click. And then the dial tone returned. She listened to the steady hum for a few seconds, then remembered that Mary was waiting on the other line. "Hello, Mary? Hi. I'm back. That was guess who."

"What did he say?" Mary asked, sitting back on the bed, the towel wrapped around her hair.

"Not much. I told him I just forgot." Joanna giggled.

"I can't believe you're being so mean. Why are you playing these games with him, Joanna? Why don't you just tell him you don't want to see him anymore?"

"Come on, Mary," Joanna chided. "It's much more fun to make him squirm for a while."

"You — you're not serious, are you?"

"No. I'm not. *Really*." Joanna couldn't decide if she was serious or not. She surprised herself at how aloof she felt about what she was doing, about how little feeling she had for Dex.

She had thought she was in love with him, after

all. But now she didn't feel much of anything at all. And deep down inside, she had to admit she did enjoy watching him squirm.

"I'd tell him straight out," she told Mary, "but you know how theatrical he is. He'd pull a big scene. Probably do the third act of *Macbeth* in my living room, have us all in tears." She laughed.

That's so cold, Mary couldn't help thinking again. I thought she cared about him. She really had me fooled. Had all of us fooled.

"I just think it'll be easier if I let him down slowly. You know, a few subtle hints. Then maybe let him see me out with Shep. That way he'll start to catch on."

"Joanna — really. You can't do that to Dex."

"Just watch me," Joanna said, admiring her dark red nail polish as she talked.

"Maybe we should change the subject," Mary said. "We've always been honest with each other, Joanna. But this time I — "

"You're right. Maybe we should change the subject." Joanna laughed, trying to keep it light, but it sounded phony even to her.

Silence for a few moments.

Finally Mary said, "Did you buy that winter coat you were looking at? The down one with the fur hood?"

"Oh, there were two I really liked," Joanna told her. "I couldn't decide which one I liked better. So I bought them both."

There was silence at the other end. Joanna

thought she heard a short gasp. She loved shocking Mary. But it wasn't much of a challenge. Mary was so simple and nice, and she shocked so easily.

"I'm so spoiled. It's disgusting, isn't it?" Joanna said.

"Yes," Mary answered quickly. "It sure is!"

"Hey, I think I hear my mother roaming the halls again — for a change. She never can sleep. I'd better get off."

"Okay. See you," Mary said.

"I'll call you tomorrow." Joanna hung up the cellular phone and returned it to its holder on her desk. She took a deep breath and stretched. She was feeling pretty good.

She listened to her mother's muffled footsteps retreat down the carpeted hallway. Poor Mom. She's always so nervous, so restless these days.

On an impulse, Joanna picked up the phone again. She looked through her directory for Shep's number.

Should I call him?

Why not?

It rang four times before someone picked it up. Silence. "Hello, Shep?"

Someone yawned loudly on the other end.

"Shep, is that you?"

"Yeah. Who is it?"

"It's me. Joanna. Did I wake you?"

Another yawn. "No. I mean, yes. I guess you did. What time is it? Hi."

They talked awkwardly for a few minutes. It didn't take Shep long to wake up.

"I'm surprised you're not out on a Friday night," Joanna said coyly.

"No. I stayed home in case you called," he cracked.

He has a good sense of humor, she thought. I like that. She decided to go ahead and ask him out. "Are you busy Saturday night?"

He seemed a little surprised by her directness. "No. I don't think so. I mean, no."

"Want to go to the movies or something?"

"I'll pick *something*," he joked. And then he added, "Hey, aren't you going with that guy from across town?"

"Well, no," she said quickly. "Not exactly."

"Great!" he said, suddenly very enthusiastic. She could picture his blond, wavy hair, his round cheeks, which made him look like such a little boy. He was probably blushing. He seemed to blush all the time, getting all rosy for no reason at all. "See you Saturday," he said.

"See you Saturday."

She was still replaying the conversation half an hour later, lying under the covers, watching the shadows of the trees outside her window shift and dip across the wall.

She couldn't have been asleep more than an hour when she was awakened by a loud clambering at the window.

She pulled herself up with a startled gasp.

Framed by pale yellow moonlight, Dex was climbing into the room.

The moonlight made his skin look green. And he had the strangest look on his face.

Joanna's breath caught in her throat.

"Dex — what do you want?" she cried.

Chapter 3

He stood by the window, eerily framed in the pale moonlight, catching his breath, staring at her across the dark room.

She pulled the satin sheet up to her chin protectively. "Dex, what are you doing here?" This is the end, she thought angrily. These middle-of-the-night visits have *got* to stop.

"It's a beautiful night," he said, still staring at her as he wiped off his hands. Climbing the tree to her second-story window was not an easy feat.

"So?"

"So come on." He flashed her his famous smile. Even in the near-darkness it was a fabulous, winning grin. "Get your car. We'll go for a ride."

"Huh? Are you crazy?"

"Yeah." He laughed. He took a few steps toward her.

"Dex, how did you get here?"

"Flew."

"Have you been drinking?"

"Yeah. I had a coupla root beers while I waited

for you at the mall. Come on — get dressed." She had left her jeans on the chair beside the bed. He picked them up and tossed them to her.

She ignored them. "You took the bus here? Doesn't your aunt know that you sneak out at night?"

"I don't know what she knows," he said. "We don't talk much."

"Well, I really don't think — "

"Stop wasting time," he said, pacing impatiently.

She suddenly saw him pacing at the mall again, looking so unhappy.

"Get dressed. Let's go for a ride. You know. Do something exciting, something no one else we know is doing. Dare to live, know what I mean?"

"Is that from a play?"

"Pete's with me," he said, ignoring her sarcasm. "He's waiting outside."

Joanna didn't really care for Dex's friend Pete. With his short, spiky hair, the diamond stud in his ear, and the heavy metal music rattling in his Walkman all the time, he was such an adolescent. What was he trying to prove — that he was cool or something?

She looked at Dex, his face half in shadow, half out.

What was I trying to prove by going with Dex? she wondered. That I was cool? That I wasn't who I am? Sure, he's handsome. Sure, he's exciting to be with in a crazy sort of way. But he's so . . . low-class. He isn't my kind at all.

Dex was my teenage rebellion phase, she decided

with sudden certainty. That's it. He was a phase I went through. Every teenager has to go through a rebellion phase, right?

"Come on, Joanna. Let's get moving! We're wasting time. What are you thinking about?"

"Nothing," she said.

"Well, all right. Get dressed. Pete's waiting. We'll drive to the Promontory. It'll be beautiful." He saw that she wasn't making a move to get up. "Just for a few minutes. Just so we can say we did it." She never could resist him when he pleaded like that, like a lost little boy.

"Well. . . ."

"And I promise I won't come here in the middle of the night anymore. Okay?"

"You promise?"

"Well . . . I won't come very often." He laughed, expecting her to laugh, too, then stopped abruptly, surprised by her hard expression. "What's wrong?"

"Nothing. Everything," she said, realizing that she was going to give in one last time, that she was going to go along on this wild escapade out to the cliffs in the middle of the night.

"I waited at the mall two hours for you," he said. "Come on. You owe me."

Now she laughed. "I owe you? Well, I guess I have no choice then." She turned and lowered her feet to the thick, shag carpet. "Do you mind turning around while I get dressed?"

"Hey, Jo — since when are you so modest?" He leered at her.

Ugh, she thought. He's so immature.

What did I ever see in him?

This is the last time I'm going anywhere with him, she thought, pulling on the jeans, then searching her dresser drawer in the darkness for a sweatshirt.

"It's so warm for October," he said.

"Spare me the weather reports," she said drily.

She didn't realize he had stepped up behind her. He put his arms around her and, turning her around, kissed her, tentatively at first, then harder.

He *does* have his good qualities, Joanna thought, returning the kiss. Then she shoved him gently away. "Pete's waiting, remember?"

"He likes to wait," Dex said, reaching for her again.

He smelled so sweet, so soapy sweet. She kissed him again.

No. This was crazy.

"Come on. I'll get the car." She pulled away from him and headed to the hallway. She grabbed her down vest, and they sneaked down the front stairs and out the front door.

Pete was waiting in the driveway, his Walkman headphones over his ears, as usual. The moonlight seemed to emphasize his bad skin. He was wearing a lightweight zippered jacket with the collar turned up. He grinned at Joanna.

She gave him a short wave and headed to the garage, pulling on the down vest. Climbing behind the wheel of the BMW, she took a deep breath. The leather smelled so good. She put the car into neutral and Dex and Pete pushed it backwards down the drive. If she started it in the garage, Joanna knew, it was certain to awaken her mother. This wasn't the first late-night drive the three of them had taken.

But it's the last, she thought, as Dex climbed in beside her, grinning excitedly, and Pete folded his long legs into the backseat. She started the car and headed toward the high cliffs at the edge of town that everyone called the Promontory.

The houses on both sides of the street were dark. There were no other cars on the road. "Turn on the radio," Pete said, leaning over the seatback. "Put on Z-190. It's Metal Maniacs Hour."

"No way, man," Dex said, lowering his window, letting in a blast of cold air. "We're listening to the quiet. Just listen to that. Beautiful, huh?"

He looked over at Joanna, who kept her eyes straight ahead on the curving white line in the middle of the road. She was more tired than she had thought, and driving was taking all of her concentration.

The houses gave way to woods, then open fields as they headed out of town. The Promontory was a popular makeout spot for Middlewood teenagers. But of course it would be deserted this time of night.

A large moving truck honked its horn as it headed past, startling Joanna. She gripped the wheel tighter as she turned onto Cliff Road, more of a gravel path than a road. The moon had disappeared behind clouds. Trees whispered and shook in the darkness.

"I feel *good*!" Dex shouted exuberantly out of the open window as the car sped over the gravel.

"Can't you close that window? It's freezing," Joanna complained.

He turned to look at her, surprised that she wasn't getting into the spirit of things. "Hey, lighten up," he said. "This is great! This is awesome!"

She didn't reply. She skidded to a stop as the gravel road abruptly ended at a low fence made of logs. A few yards beyond the fence, the high granite cliffs jutted out, overlooking the town.

Dex leaped out of the car, shouting up at the sky.

"Hey — you forgot to close your door!" Joanna called angrily after him. But he didn't hear her. He was already half running, half skipping to the cliff edge.

Pete climbed out of the back, tinny drum rhythms escaping from his headphones. Joanna held the car key in her hand, thinking about locking the car, then decided it was silly. No one else would be foolish enough to be up here at three o'clock in the morning.

She walked around to the other side of the car, the ground soft and wet beneath her sneakers, and closed Dex's door. Then, dropping the car keys in her vest pocket, she started walking slowly toward Dex on the cliff edge.

"Hey, it's a lot colder up here," she complained,

snapping her vest as the cold wind gusted about her.

"It's great!" Dex called, a dark shadow against a darker sky. "Come here! Take a look!"

She shivered. Was it the cold? Or the cliff edge? She had always had a problem with heights.

He took her hand and pulled her close to him. "Look — the whole town." He pointed.

"It's all dark," she said without enthusiasm. "All of the smart people are asleep."

His arm tightened around her waist. "Hey, you're a lot of laughs tonight," he said softly, bringing his face close to hers.

"It's too cold. I thought it was warmer out," she said.

"I'll warm you up." He squeezed her waist again.

She looked for Pete. He was off by himself several yards down, sitting on a large rock, staring down into the dark valley that held the town, his foot tapping to the music that pounded in his ears.

Why am I here with them? Joanna asked herself, as a strong blast of wind pushed her toward the jagged cliff edge. Why aren't I home asleep, safe in my bed, like every sane person in town?

She thought of her mother padding around the halls at all hours, unable to sleep. What if her mother happened to look into Joanna's bedroom and see that Joanna was gone? I'd be history, Joanna thought with a shudder. I'd be dead meat. She wouldn't let me out of her sight for the next decade!

And then I couldn't go out with Shep on Saturday night. . . .

"Hey, Dex — what are you doing?" Her voice caught in her throat. She looked up to see him standing ostrichlike on one leg at the very edge of the cliff.

"Just trying to get your attention," he said, laughing. "You seem to be somewhere else tonight."

"Dex — stop it! You're frightening me!"

"All right!" he cried. "I think I finally *do* have your attention! Now, for my next trick. . . ." He started hopping up and down on the one foot, his other foot stretched up in the air behind him.

"No, please! Stop! You'll fall!"

And as Joanna said the word, Dex slipped and fell over the edge.

Chapter 4

The sky seemed to blacken. The ground started to spin.

"Dex?"

She blinked her eyes, then opened them wide, thinking that when she opened them, he'd be back where he had been, standing on one foot, hopping up and down on the cliff edge.

But there was only darkness.

"Dex?"

Her heart felt as if it had stopped beating. She wasn't sure she could breathe.

She took a step to the edge. But she was too dizzy.

"Dex?"

He poked his head up from below the surface, a wide, delighted grin on his face. "Gotcha!"

She just stared at him open-mouthed. She couldn't speak.

He laughed. "Aren't you going to help me up?"

"You — you — "

"It was a gag." He reached his arms over the rock surface and started to pull himself up. "There's a little ledge here. Fooled you, huh?" He looked up at her expectantly.

"You creep," she muttered angrily, her heart beginning to beat again.

"See? You really do care!" he said, laughing.

"That wasn't funny, Dex."

"It wasn't really supposed to be funny," he said, pulling himself all the way up, standing up with a groan, and dusting off his jeans. "I guess it was like . . . performance art."

She made a disgusted face and turned away.

"Hey — what's wrong?" he asked, coming toward her. "You always used to enjoy my little performances."

"Well, I didn't enjoy this one!"

"Hey — what's going on?" Pete called from across the darkness. He had lit a cigarette, and all she could see was the glow of it.

"Huh? You missed it?" Dex called, disappointed.

"Missed what?"

"Never mind," Joanna said quickly. She no longer felt upset or frightened. Her anger had forced away those feelings. What a stupid, mean trick to pull!

"Hey, watch! I'll show you!" Dex yelled.

Pete stood up to get a better view.

A gust of wind battered all three of them. "Stop it, Dex!" Joanna cried. She turned and started going toward the car. "I'm leaving. Are you two coming with me?"

"One second," Dex said, holding up one finger. "I just have to do my little performance for Pete. Now watch carefully — "

"No — don't!" Joanna screamed. "I mean it, Dex! It wasn't funny the first time. It was horrible! I'll never speak to you again if — "

"You'll like it better the second time," Dex said, looking to see if Pete was watching.

"Dex — I'm warning you!" Joanna took another few steps toward the car. Her sneakers were soaked through from the wet ground. She felt cold and uncomfortable. "Are you coming?"

She turned back to see Dex back on the cliff edge, balancing again on one foot. "Ta-daa!" he cried, a gleeful smile on his face.

The smile suddenly faded as Dex's eyes opened wide in horror.

Joanna saw his expression change. Then she looked down and saw why.

A large chunk of stone was crumbling beneath Dex. The cliff edge was breaking away.

"No! No!"

He threw his arms up as he began to drop and frantically grabbed for the edge. But it crumbled in his hands.

"No — Dex!"

His head disappeared, and then his flailing hands.

She heard his body hit hard against the side.

"No — Dex!"

She heard him scream all the way down.

Then from down below she heard a cracking sound, the sound of eggs breaking.

This wasn't a joke.

This wasn't a performance.

This was real.

This was a death.

Joanna didn't even realize she was running until she reached the car.

She could hear Pete calling to her, his voice high-pitched and frightened, but she couldn't make out the words over the siren of her panic. The siren was drowning out everything. It seemed to echo between her ears, so loud, so unbearably loud.

She couldn't think.

She couldn't hear.

Was Pete calling to her? Was she running away? Was she climbing into the car, fumbling in her vest pocket for the car key?

"Joanna — come back!"

She couldn't hear anything. The siren had taken over her brain.

"We've got to help him! Joanna! Come back!"

What was he saying?

Come back?

But how could she?

If she stayed, her mother would find out she had sneaked out. Her mother would find out everything. Everyone in town would know what she had done.

How could she stay?

Her mother would take away her car. Take away her charge cards. Take away . . . everything.

For Dex?

Stay and have her life ruined for Dex?

She'd stay — if it weren't already too late.

But she heard him fall. She heard the horrifying sound when he hit the bottom.

She'd probably be hearing it for the rest of her life.

No. No way. No way, Dex.

Poor, dead Dex.

"Joanna — come back! We've got to help him! We've got to save him!"

Help him?

Is that what Pete was yelling?

The siren was just so loud, so overwhelmingly loud. Maybe if I drive real fast, the siren will go away.

The car was already in reverse. She was already backing away from the low fence.

No way. No way, Dex.

I can't ruin my life for you. I was going to break up with you, anyway. Don't you see? You're just not right for me. You're just not my kind. You understand, don't you?

Don't you?

The tires squealed as she floored the gas pedal, and the car began to race over the gravel road, slipping from side to side, noisily spitting a tidal wave of gravel behind it.

Lose my car? Lose my . . . reputation?

Shep's face flashed into her mind. He looked so good to her. So safe.

Sorry, Dex.

I'll get help.

Don't worry. I'm not abandoning you. I'll get help.

That's what she'd do. As soon as she got home, she'd dial 911. She'd tell them to hurry to the Promontory.

She'd save Dex after all.

She wasn't running away. She was running for help.

She started to feel better. The siren faded to a low, insistent wail.

I'm getting help. Pete will understand.

I'm getting help.

The tires squealed as she turned onto the Town Road. She realized she was going too fast.

But I have to go fast. I'm getting help for Dex.

As soon as I get home.

As soon as I can.

She didn't see the truck until it was too late.

She saw the lights first. She wondered why she was suddenly bathed in light.

She thought it might not be real. It might be part of her panic, like the siren.

But the lights grew brighter.

They were truck headlights. The truck swerved to avoid her, but the road was too narrow.

By the time Joanna realized she was about to be hit head-on, it was too late to react.

The lights grew brighter, brighter, seemed to surround her.

Everything was glowing.

And then the siren was drowned out by the sound of breaking glass and bending steel.

And the lights gave way to darkness.

Chapter 5

The blackness lightened to a murky gray. Shadows in a dark fog. Clouds. Heavy, gray clouds. Then nothing at all.

She opened her eyes.

The room was a blur. A dark, warm blur. It was very still. Unearthly still.

The quiet is deafening, she thought.

And then she realized she was awake. And the room, coming quickly into focus, was her bedroom. She happily recognized the light through the open window, the shadows from the trees on the familiar flowered wallpaper. The two framed Picasso prints over the bookshelf next to the desk.

Home. She was home.

She raised her head, testing it. She raised her left arm, then her right. She stretched.

I don't hurt. I'm okay.

She sat up quickly.

I feel fine.

I must be dreaming. She yawned. No. The truck

was a dream. The headlights, those blinding, yellow headlights weren't real. The accident wasn't real. It never happened.

I'm fine.

She pushed down the bedspread and the satin sheet and started to climb out of bed. But a sudden fluttering at the window made her stop.

Just the curtains?

No. She heard a scrabbling against the side of the house, a soft thud.

That's odd, she thought, pulling the sheet back up. Why is the window wide open in October?

There were other things that puzzled her. The quiet was one of them. Except for the soft thuds outside, it was so eerily quiet.

Where was her mother? Why wasn't she waiting at her bedside for her to awaken?

Because there was no accident, she told herself. Because it was all a dream.

A dark form filled the window. It moved quickly, struggling, pulling itself into the room, one leg, one arm, then another leg. It stepped into the square of moonlight.

"Dex!" she cried.

"Ssshhh." He raised his finger to his lips, his eyes glowing like dark jewels.

"Dex — you're okay!" We're both okay, she thought.

His smile seemed to warm the room. "It's a beautiful night," he whispered. "Come on, get dressed. Let's go for a walk."

"A walk?"

She wondered what time it was, what day. How had she gotten back to bed?

She had to remind herself that she had been in bed all along. In bed dreaming a terrible dream.

"Okay." She rose quickly, feeling light as air, and floated across the room to pull a designer running suit from her dresser drawer.

"Hurry," he whispered, sounding very excited and happy.

She was dressed in an instant, headed for the door, then hesitated. She walked over to Dex, grabbed his arm, squeezed it hard.

He was real.

He was really there.

He laughed. "What's the matter with you?"

"Nothing," she said. Why go into it?

She remembered that she had decided to break up with him, not to see him anymore. I'll have to tell him, she thought. It won't be easy, but I'll have to tell him. Maybe I'll tell him during our walk.

They were outside now, and starting to jog. It felt so good to be moving, to feel the cool wind on her face.

She jogged a little faster, leaving Dex behind.

"Hey, wait up!"

He'll always be a little behind me, she thought. He'll never really be able to catch up.

It was still so silent. The silence was almost *thick*.

It must have been very late. No cars moved. The houses were dark. The wind blew but the trees didn't move. The fallen brown leaves, scattered all over the ground, stayed in place as if nailed down.

Strange.

Joanna jogged a little faster.

"Hey — " Dex called from several yards behind.

She didn't turn around. It felt so good to run, to move, to be okay.

"Hey — "

She looked back without slowing her pace. She was running really fast now, and not the least bit out of breath.

"Hey — "

Dex, she realized, looked angry. What was his problem?

She turned again. A streetlight cast a cone of white light down on him. His eyes were narrowed, his mouth pulled back in an angry frown.

He looks frightening, Joanna thought.

And her next thought frightened her even more: He's not running with me anymore. He's chasing me.

"Hey!"

She knew she was right. She picked up speed. She glanced quickly back. Dex picked up speed, too.

He was gaining on her.

Why was he doing this? Why did he look so frightening, so angry? She wanted to stop. But she was afraid.

Where were they?

The houses were gone. The woods gave way to flat fields. She could see low, black hills against the purple night sky.

How far have we run? It doesn't seem as if we've been running that long.

"Hey — you — "

His voice sounded so angry, so filled with hatred.

He's going to catch me, she thought, feeling her legs begin to ache, feeling her chest begin to heave for breath. He's going to catch me, and then —

And then?

A cold shudder ran down her body.

She forced herself to run harder. Every step hurt now, every thrust of her legs sent a flash of pain up her back. But she knew she had to keep running.

"Joanna — stop!"

She ignored his angry call, gulped in a mouthful of air, and ran, her sneakers sinking into the wet ground.

Ground?

Where were they?

The ground seemed to dip, then rise again. The soft ground gave way to granite.

The Promontory.

They had run to the Promontory. He had chased her to the Promontory. Had this been his destination all along?

She was only a few dozen yards from the cliff edge. She stopped, gasping for breath, her entire body throbbing, pulsing with pain. She spun around.

"Dex — stop!"

He came running right at her, his expression fixed in hatred.

"Dex — why are you doing this?"

He seemed to pick up speed rather than slow down. He was only a few yards away now. His dark eyes burned into hers. His mouth opened wide, and he tossed his head back in a silent scream.

"Dex — stop! *Please!*"

He ran past her, ran right over the cliff edge. His legs scissored in midair. His hands flailed wildly above his head. He spun, turned to face her, an accusing look on his face. Then he started to drop.

It was Joanna's turn to scream. She closed her eyes tight and tossed back her head, and screamed and screamed.

No sound came out.

When she opened her eyes, she was in a very bright, white room.

Her mother's face loomed over her.

Joanna could see the crisscross of lines at the corners of her mother's eyes, the small pores of her made-up cheeks, the crumbs of orange lipstick on her lips. She could see her mother's face so clearly. There was a damp path down the makeup on her cheeks where tears must have recently trickled.

Her mother's smile was broad. Too broad.

"She's coming out of it now," a woman's voice said from somewhere behind her mother.

"It's starting to wear off," another woman said.

Her mother's smile grew even wider. She leaned down over Joanna until they almost touched noses.

"What?" Joanna asked.

"She'll be fully awake soon," one of the unseen women said.

"She did very well," the other added in a hushed tone.

Her mother's face didn't move. It hovered above Joanna like a pink balloon.

I'm still dreaming, Joanna thought.

"You're going to be fine," her mother said, her smile still fixed. The face retreated a little. Tears formed near the tangled crisscross of age lines.

Yes, I'm going to be fine because I'm still dreaming.

She tried to sit up.

Everything hurt.

I'm paralyzed, she thought, and the sweet calmness of the dream sensation gave way to panic.

"Hey — "

"You're going to be fine," her mother said softly. The tears ran down the already defined tracks on her cheeks.

I don't believe you, Joanna thought.

She struggled to sit up. When that didn't prove possible, she struggled to move her arms. That wasn't possible, either.

"Help — Mom — "

"She's fully awake now," a voice said.

"That's a good sign," the other voice added.

Who *are* those women? Joanna wondered angrily.

"Don't try to move," her mother said.

"I can't," Joanna told her, her voice tiny, like a baby's voice.

I'm a baby again, she thought. I was just born again.

Crazy thought.

I've been drugged or something.

A crazy thought that was probably true.

She looked past her mother with her frozen, tear-stained smile to the white tile walls, the bright fluorescent lights, the white-uniformed nurses standing side by side in the doorway.

I'm in a hospital.

And I'm not dreaming now.

It all seemed too much to gather in. It was taking all of her strength, all of her concentration to *see*.

"You're going to be fine," her mother repeated, like a song chorus.

You always were a bad liar, Joanna thought.

She hated the smell of her mother's makeup. So orangey. So ugly.

She drifted back to sleep with the smell clinging to her nostrils.

"She needs to sleep," a nearby voice said.

"You really were lucky," her mother said, a few days later. She sat stiffly in a folding chair beside the hospital bed, her fur coat on her lap. "Your beautiful face wasn't touched."

"Just about everything else was," Joanna groaned.

"Joanna, really. Don't complain. A truck like that. You could have been — you could have been. . . ." She bit her trembling lower lip. "A few broken bones. Really, dear. You should be so grateful."

"Yeah. Grateful," Joanna repeated.

Whatever painkillers they were feeding into her arm made her feel as if she were not completely in the room. She felt as if she had traded places with her shadow. Her shadow lay braced and bandaged on this hard hospital bed. Her real body — and her mind — were off somewhere else.

She was continually drifting off to sleep, sometimes in the middle of conversations. She wasn't allowed visitors yet, only her mother. The visits tired her out. She wished her mother would stop staring at her so intensely. She wished they would stop pumping stuff into her, so that she could think straight.

"In another few weeks, you'll be strong enough to begin therapy for your leg," Mrs. Collier said matter-of-factly.

"Yeah. Well, I'm so grateful for that, too," Joanna said sarcastically.

"Just stop it, Joanna. Let's take this one day at a time."

"Don't you mean one *cliché* at a time?" Joanna cracked, knowing she was giving her mother a hard time and not caring.

"This has all been such a terrible shock for all of us," Mrs. Collier said, deciding to ignore her daughter's sarcasm. "When I got that call from the police at three in the morning that you — that you were in an accident and — "

Joanna realized she hadn't explained a thing to her mother.

"What were you doing out, Joanna? Why did you sneak out of the house?"

She just didn't have the strength to get into it now. Drifting halfway between the real world and the shadowy world induced by the painkillers, she hadn't even thought about that horrible night.

Hadn't even thought about Dex.

She drifted off to sleep, wondering how she would ever explain.

"Pete?"

Joanna tried to sit up, then remembered that she couldn't. She looked for her mother, but she wasn't there. It was Pete sitting awkwardly in the folding chair now.

His face was flushed. His eyes darted nervously from her face to the floor. His hands were clasped tightly in his lap.

"Pete?"

"Hi, Joanna. Are you awake? I mean — "

"No. I'm talking in my sleep. Pete, are you okay?"

"Yeah. Fine." His face turned a little brighter red. "Your mom says you're going to be fine."

"She says it four hundred times a day," Joanna said bitterly, rolling her eyes. They were the only part of her she could move without any pain. "So it's got to be a lie."

Pete just stared at her. "You're pretty beat-up, huh?"

She laughed a dry laugh. It made her broken ribs hurt. "Good question, Pete. Got any others?"

He pulled at the diamond stud in his ear.

They sat in silence for a while. He stared at her. She had the feeling that he was waiting for something.

Finally he broke the silence. "Aren't you going to ask me about Dex?" He asked it angrily, accusingly.

What's wrong with me? Joanna wondered. Why *didn't* I ask about Dex? Is it just these awful drugs? Am I losing my mind? Am I trying to shut out all memories of that night?

"Well, Dex died," Pete said, shouting now. He jumped to his feet, his face filled with disgust. "Dex died, Joanna. He didn't make it. He died that night. And you couldn't even bother to ask me about him."

Chapter 6

Mary came to visit a few days later. Or was it the same day? Joanna couldn't keep track of time, didn't even try.

"Sssh. I brought you something," Mary said, whispering, acting very secretive as she dug in the big, floppy embroidered bag she always carried.

"I like your hair," Joanna said.

"My hair? I didn't even brush it." She continued to rummage in the bag. "Here it is." She looked behind her to the door to make sure no one was coming in.

Joanna laughed at the secrecy. "Mary — what on earth — ?"

Mary handed her a Snickers bar. "Quick — hide it."

"A Snickers bar? Mary — I'm touched!"

"Just hide it," Mary insisted, "before they take it away from you. I figured this is probably the one time you won't be watching your weight."

"What a thoughtful present," Joanna said, slipping the candy bar under the sheet.

The girls talked, animatedly at first, then awkwardly in fits and starts. They both realized that they had less to talk about now that they didn't go to the same school or have the same friends.

They talked about Joanna's broken bones, and about how her mother was taking it all. And they talked about Mary's classes and a boy she had met at the mall.

Then, as if she had been leading up to it all along, Mary said, "Pete told me about . . . Dex."

"Yeah," Joanna said, reaching over to adjust the tube that still was stuck to her wrist.

"It — it must be so hard for you," Mary said, staring hard into Joanna's eyes, searching for something there.

"Yeah. Well . . ." Joanna didn't know what Mary expected her to say. And why was she staring at her so intensely?

The silence grew really awkward. "I wish I felt more," Joanna said, mainly to fill the silence.

"Huh? What do you mean?" Mary looked very surprised.

"I mean, it's so awful. When Pete told me that Dex was dead, my first reaction was, Now I don't have to break up with him."

Mary's mouth dropped open. "Really? That's really the first thing you thought?"

Uh-oh. I've gone too far, Joanna thought. I've been too honest. I should have known better. I should have known that would shock Mary.

It shocks me, too, in a way.

"You really didn't feel *anything*?" Mary asked, shifting uncomfortably on the small folding chair, her hands playing with the folds of her bag.

"I guess it just hasn't sunk in," Joanna said, beginning to feel tired again, wishing Mary would just leave.

"Oh."

"I mean, I'm just numb, I guess. You know. From the painkillers and stuff. I'll feel it later. I'm sure."

Mary just stared at her, much the way Pete had.

"Well, I know it sounds a little cold — " Joanna started to say, and then decided she had nothing to be defensive about.

My feelings are my own business, she told herself. I don't have to explain how I feel to Mary, or Pete, or anyone else. I'm the one who saw Dex die, after all. I'm the one who saw him fall off the cliff. I'm the one who saw the look on his face when he knew he was falling.

That's horrible enough for one lifetime.

You ran away, a voice inside her said. You didn't help him. You ran away.

I hurried to get help, was Joanna's reply to herself. I would've gotten help for him if that truck hadn't . . .

Who cares? Dex is dead, and I'm lying here wrecked.

Who cares?

Stop staring at me like I'm some disgusting kind of cold fish.

As if reading Joanna's thoughts, Mary jumped to her feet. "I've got to get going. I didn't realize how late it was."

She didn't even look at her watch, thought Joanna. She has no idea how late it is. "Thanks for coming," she said.

"Feel better," Mary said. "Get some rest."

"What else can I do?"

Mary laughed, a nervous giggle. "I'll come back sometime. I mean, when I can. 'Bye." She hurried out of the room without looking back.

"What was it — something I said?" Joanna asked aloud.

She settled her head back on the pillow.

"So what? So what? So *what*? Sorry, Dex. But so what?"

"You're not going to study tonight, are you, Joanna?"

"No, Mom. I was just carrying these books up to my room. I have a date tonight."

"Oh, I'm glad." Her mother collapsed wearily into the oversized living room armchair and raised her feet onto the ottoman. "You've been working so hard, I've been a little worried about you."

"Well, I missed six weeks of school, you know."

"I'm very pleased by how well you're doing, Joanna," Mrs. Collier said, raising her feet to examine her ankles, which were swollen. "The therapist says your leg is coming along so nicely, you can probably quit by Christmas time."

"Maybe people will stop thinking of me as 'The Gimp,'" Joanna said, and started out of the living room, forcing herself to walk without a limp, even though her leg really throbbed with pain.

"I haven't seen Mary around in quite a while," Mrs. Collier said, not noticing that Joanna was trying to leave. "Did she come visit you in the hospital?"

"Yeah. Once," Joanna said, allowing more bitterness to escape than she had intended. She quickly added, "I guess she's just real busy. It's hard, you know, to keep up with kids from other schools."

She started to leave the room again, but again her mother refused to let the conversation end. "And what about Dex?" she asked. "Did you say you were meeting him tonight? I haven't seen him once the whole time you . . ."

Joanna uttered a silent gasp. Her mother kept talking, but her voice seemed to fade as if someone had turned down the volume control.

I never told her, Joanna realized.

She never asked anything about Dex, and I never told her. She doesn't know a thing. She doesn't know that Dex is dead. Doesn't know why I was out in the middle of the night. Doesn't know anything.

And doesn't really *want* to know.

Any other mother would have demanded an explanation, Joanna told herself. Any other mother would have wanted to know every detail.

Maybe I'm lucky.

Lucky that she doesn't care enough to ask.

I don't care, either.

So, we're both lucky.

"I'm not seeing Dex anymore," she said, finding it easy to keep her voice flat and emotionless.

"Really?"

Mrs. Collier was trying to play it cool. But Joanna knew how much that news would thrill her. Her mother never could stand Dex, mainly for the same reasons that had Joanna planning to break up with him.

"I have a date with Shep tonight," Joanna said.

"Shephard Forrest?"

Joanna nodded.

"Hilda Forrest's son? How nice." A pleased smile formed on Mrs. Collier's face.

"I'm glad you approve," Joanna snapped. It bothered her to see her mother so happy.

"I didn't mean — Well . . . it's just that Shephard is much more appropriate."

"Appropriate?" Joanna laughed, a scornful laugh. "What a word!"

Why am I giving my mother such a hard time? she wondered. I *agree* with her that Shep is more appropriate.

It's just not her place to say it.

I should tell her that Dex fell off a cliff and died. Just to see her squirm. Just to see her come up with an *appropriate* response.

But instead, she shifted the books she'd been

carrying to her other arm, and walked quickly up to her room to get ready for her date with Shep.

"I love that sweater, Shep," Joanna said. "Is it cashmere?"

"I guess. I'll let you touch it if you wash your hands first." He gave her that adorable lopsided grin, the one that made the dimple appear in his left cheek.

She laughed and rubbed the sleeve of the pale blue sweater. "Yep. It's cashmere."

"My grandmother gave it to me," Shep said, blushing a little as Joanna kept her hand on his arm.

He had insisted on taking her to the winter dance at Garland High, the public high school he had attended before switching to Landover. "It'll be a goof," he said.

Joanna didn't know any of the kids there, and the whole idea of going to a dance at a public high school seemed like a real downer to her, but she didn't want Shep to think she was a bad sport, so she agreed with a smile.

"Maybe I should dress down a bit," she had said when he told her his plans for the evening after arriving at her house. She was wearing a maroon silk blouse and a dark suede miniskirt over black tights.

"I think you look okay," he said, a little uncomfortably.

She liked his shyness. He was so incredibly good-looking, she thought, a little shyness made him more human.

"Shall we take my car?" she asked. She was so accustomed to driving Dex around, the question came automatically.

"No way," he said. "Look." He led her to her front door and pointed to the drive. Basking in the light from the porch was a brand-new silver Jaguar.

Joanna's mouth dropped open. "It's yours?"

"My grandmother gave it to me." He was grinning now. He ran a hand back quickly through his wavy, blond hair.

"*Nice* grandmother!" Joanna exclaimed.

"Well, she's very old and very rich," Shep said seriously. "And very lonely. And I'm her only grandson."

"Lucky you," Joanna said, resting her hand on his arm again. "I guess we'll be going in style to the Garland High hop!"

When they got to the Garland High gym, everyone seemed so glad to see Shep. A steady stream of kids kept coming up to greet him and ask him how he was doing at Landover, and if he missed all of his friends at Garland.

Shep seemed right at home with these kids. I thought this was supposed to be a goof, Joanna thought, a little resentfully, seeing how excited and pleased Shep was to be back here. "Good lord — look at that girl's outfit," she said, pointing to a girl in a brown, fringed skirt and white plastic boots. "How tacky."

"I think it's kind of sexy," Shep said, almost defensively.

"They could have spent a few dollars to decorate

the place a little better," Joanna griped. "I mean balloons and crepe paper streamers? Get real!"

But to her surprise, Shep didn't join in her laughter. "It doesn't look so bad. You know, they can't afford to have their dances at a hotel ballroom, the way we do at Landover. Everyone seems to be having a good time, anyway, don't you think?"

Joanna quickly agreed. "Yeah, it's great," she said, trying not to sound as unenthusiastic as she felt. "Oh, no! Look at that girl's hair! Unbelievable!"

Shep looked at her, an odd smile on his face. "Joanna, you're such a snob." He said it jokingly, but there was definitely a tone of disapproval in it.

I'd better be careful, Joanna thought. Shep doesn't seem to appreciate my sense of humor.

She danced with him to the blaring music over the terrible loudspeakers and tried to join in shouted conversations with his friends, who seemed pretty nice. It was about eleven o'clock when she asked to leave for the first time. And by eleven-thirty, he had said good-bye to everyone, and they were walking across the street to the car.

"I told you it would be a goof," he said, his arm casually around her shoulders. His coat smelled like the gym.

Mine probably does, too, Joanna thought unhappily. "Yeah. I like your friends," she said, working hard to sound genuine and enthusiastic.

She sat very close to him as he drove her home. A heavy frost had settled over the lawns. As they drove past, the ground looked silvery white, as if it had snowed. She nestled her head against his shoulder, looking up to see if he seemed pleased by it.

"You want to go to a movie or something next weekend?" he asked, his eyes straight ahead on the road.

"Yeah. I would," she said softly, secretly feeling as if she had scored a victory. Shep was hooked, definitely hooked.

She inhaled deeply. "I just love the smell of a new car," she said happily.

He kissed her good night at her door. He started to end the kiss, but she grabbed the back of his head with both hands and pulled him back, pressing her lips against his in a long, lingering kiss. Finally he headed back to his car, a goofy grin on his handsome face.

She stood and watched him get into the car. He pressed down on the gas, making the engine roar, the blast of exhaust white against the darkness of the night. Then he backed silently away.

Score one for Joanna, she thought, as she turned the lock and entered the house. He's just right for me. A little lacking in the sense-of-humor area, maybe. But he can be shaped up.

She hurried up to her room and was getting undressed when her cellular phone rang. She glanced at the clock. It was a few minutes after midnight.

Who could it be?

She picked it up after the second ring, her arm tangled in the sleeve of her blouse. "Hello?"

She heard crackling at the other end. It was either a bad connection or someone was calling long distance.

"Hello?" she repeated, a little louder.

"Hi, Joanna." A boy's voice, sounding very far away. "It's me."

"What?"

"Joanna — it's me. Dex. How you doin'?"

Chapter 7

Joanna didn't reply.

She dropped the phone back into its holder.

The voice. It *was* Dex's voice, she thought.

But that's impossible. Of course, that's impossible.

Someone was playing a cruel trick on her. But who could it be?

Who could sound so much like Dex? Who would want to scare Joanna, to make her feel bad?

Pete?

Was it Pete? She hadn't seen Pete since that day in the hospital. Since the day Pete had come to tell her that Dex was dead.

Pete was so angry at her, Joanna remembered, so shocked that she hadn't asked about Dex immediately. So outraged when Joanna didn't cry at the horrible news.

Outraged. That was the only word to describe it.

Pete was the only one who knew that she had

run away from the Promontory that night, that she hadn't stayed to try to rescue Dex.

But I didn't run away, she insisted to herself.

I drove away as quickly as I could to get help.

She wished she had had a chance to explain that to Pete.

That creep. She never had liked him. He was so ugly with that pockmarked face, and that awful spiky hair.

He was just stupid enough to make that phone call and pretend to be Dex.

But she knew it couldn't be Pete. Pete had such a high-pitched, scratchy voice. There was no way he could sound so much like Dex.

So exactly like Dex.

She shivered, and realized she was still undressed. She hurried over to her closet, stepping over her clothes, which she had tossed on the floor, and pulled out her warmest flannel nightshirt.

What is going on? Who would play such a stupid, mean joke?

The question repeated in her mind. She just couldn't answer it.

It took hours to fall asleep. And then she slept fitfully, waking up every few hours, thinking the phone was ringing.

Sunday was spent doing homework and watching endless, boring old movies full of stupid romance on TV.

She thought maybe Shep would call, but he didn't. So she called him after dinner, and they had a nice, short chat.

He's never asked me about Dex, she realized. Of course, he never knew Dex. But he did know that I'd been going with someone for a long time.

And he's never really asked about my accident, either.

That's strange.

Maybe he just doesn't like to bring up unpleasant subjects, she thought. A lot of people are like that.

The next day was a blustery, cold day that showed winter was getting serious. Low, gray clouds hovered overhead as she headed home in the late afternoon after her French tutorial. Even though it was still afternoon, it was as dark as night, an eerie, heavy darkness that made it feel as if it might start to snow at any minute.

I wish I had the car, she thought, even though her French tutor lived only a couple of blocks from her house. She pulled the fur hood of her coat up, and picked up her pace. The cold made her foot throb, but she forced herself not to limp. Any change in the weather made her foot and ribs and shoulders ache. It was just something she was going to have to live with, she realized.

As she approached Trafalgar Avenue, the street-lights flickered and came on. The sudden light startled her. It made everything suddenly look different. New shadows shifted and played across the sidewalk.

It took Joanna a few seconds to realize what had happened. She stared up at the street lamp above her head, and for a split second, the yellow light reminded her of the truck headlights, the truck headlights that had seemed to grow and grow, widen and widen until they were all around her.

With a silent gasp, she looked away quickly, turning her gaze across Trafalgar, one of the busiest avenues in Middlewood.

Leaning against a bus-stop post across the street, illuminated by a circle of yellow light from a street lamp behind him, she saw a young man staring at her.

"Dex?"

He didn't move.

She froze.

She recognized the red windbreaker. He had worn it a million times.

"Dex?"

The traffic light was against her. A steady stream of cars poured down Trafalgar, people on their way home from work.

Except for the windbreaker, he seemed all yellow and black, bathed in the light from the street lamp.

He stared at her, unmoving. And she stared back.

It can't be.

It's impossible.

Dex, you're dead.

She knew her eyes were playing tricks on her. It had to be another boy, another boy with black hair, bold, black eyes, and a red windbreaker. Another boy who leaned just like Dex.

Who looked just like Dex.

She heard his voice again, the voice on the phone

Saturday night. "Hi, it's me. How you doin'?"

The voice from so far away.

The light changed.

He didn't move. He leaned against the narrow yellow post, staring straight ahead at her. She shivered. Not from the cold.

She had to know the truth.

"Dex?"

She started across the street. But a city bus ran the red light, roaring through the intersection.

Joanna leaped back to the curb, startled.

When the bus had passed, she looked across the street.

Dex was gone.

Chapter 8

Joanna rolled over with a weary groan and tugged hard at the covers. The bottom of the sheet pulled out from under the mattress. She sat up. Now I'll have to remake the bed, she thought. She couldn't stand to have her feet sticking out from under the covers.

She stood up in the darkness and glanced at the clock on her desk. Twelve-fifteen.

Why can't I get to sleep?

It was chilly in the room, even in her flannel nightshirt. Maybe I should close the window, she thought. She pulled the sheet down and tucked it in. Out on the street a car drove by, its radio blaring country music.

I'll never get to sleep, Joanna thought, climbing back under the covers. I'm not even sleepy. Maybe I should get up and work on my book report.

The scrabbling sounds outside the window made her sit up with a start. She heard scraping noises. Sneakers against the tree trunk.

No.

It wasn't possible.

She had to be imagining it. The way she had imagined seeing Dex standing on that street corner.

She uttered a soft cry as a hand grabbed the window ledge from outside. A head popped up, hidden in shadow.

No.

Joanna gripped the edge of the bedspread, pulling it up to her chin as if to shield herself.

She leaned over and, her hand trembling, struggled to turn on the bed-table lamp. She nearly knocked it over, finally managing to click it on just as Dex pulled himself into the room.

He grinned at her, that warm, familiar grin, and walked stiffly away from the window into the yellow light. He was wearing black, straight-legged jeans and a worn, leather bomber jacket. "Hi, Joanna." His voice was a whisper, almost ghostly.

"Dex?"

"Yeah. It's me."

Don't scream, don't scream, don't scream.

She realized that she'd been holding her breath. The bedspread was still pulled up to her chin.

"But — "

"How are you?" Still a whisper.

He looked pale in the yellow light, and thin. He took a few steps toward her, limping slightly, holding his left leg stiffly.

"But — Dex — you're dead!"

Joanna didn't recognize her own voice. Her

throat felt so tight, it was hard to breathe. She suddenly felt cold all over.

Don't scream, don't scream, don't scream.

"Huh?" His mouth dropped open. His face filled with surprise. He shook his long, wavy hair as if shaking off her words.

Joanna gripped the bedspread, staring into his bewildered face. He looks different, she thought. So thin, almost wasted away.

"What did you say?"

She coughed. Her throat felt tight and dry. "Dead," she said, the word sounding odd, not sounding like a real word. "Pete said you were dead, Dex."

"Huh? Really?"

He looked stunned. He pulled out the desk chair, turned it around, and sat down on it backwards, leaning his chin against the chairback. "He said I was dead?"

"Yeah. He told me. He said you didn't make it. That you — "

"But why would Pete say that?" He gripped the back of the chair and made it rock back and forth.

He's alive, she thought, starting to calm down, starting to get over the shock of seeing him climb into her room again. He's alive. He's really sitting there.

To her surprise, she realized she had mixed feelings about seeing him, sitting there, rocking the desk chair up and down. She had gotten used to the idea of him being dead.

Am I glad to see him? she asked herself.

Not really.

Mainly, she realized, seeing him made her feel less guilty.

"Yeah," she said, loosening her grip on the bedspread. "Why *did* Pete tell me that?" Her shock was beginning to turn to anger. "Was that some sort of stupid joke he was trying to pull?"

"Poor guy," Dex said softly, staring down at the plush carpet, not picking up on Joanna's anger. "He must've been in shock. He was so upset about — about what happened that night."

"He was so upset, he *thought* you were dead?" Joanna pulled herself up and leaned against the headboard. Why did she feel so cold? The room seemed to grow even colder after Dex entered.

"I guess," Dex said. A sad expression crossed his face, an expression she had never seen before.

It's not just sad, she thought. It's mournful.

"Well, where were you for the past two months?" she asked. The question came out more angry than concerned.

Her tone seemed to surprise him. "I was banged up really bad," he said, looking into her eyes. She noticed that he was holding his left leg stiff, straight out in front of him. "I had a lot of broken bones, some internal bleeding and stuff. They took me to a hospital upstate. I've been there the whole time."

"I'm sorry," she said.

You're supposed to be dead, she thought.

I felt so bad. I felt so guilty. Why did I have to go through all that for nothing?

Why did Pete do that? Out of spite? Out of anger? Did he do it for revenge, because I left him there that night?

"I wanted to call you," Dex said. "But my hands were bandaged. I looked like a mummy. My aunt tried to call, but there was never an answer at your house. Maybe she was trying the wrong number. She isn't too swift these days."

He shifted uncomfortably on the small chair. "It was so terrible, so unbearable," he said in a low, flat voice. "All the time in the hospital. All those weeks. Know what I did? I pretended I was in a play, that I was just playing a role, that it wasn't really happening to me. Pretty pathetic, huh?"

"You look good," she said, ignoring his question, looking him up and down.

You look like a skeleton, she thought.

"So you really thought I was dead?" He scratched his head. A grin crossed his face for some reason. "That explains it, I guess."

"Explains what?"

"Why I never heard from you. Why you never visited. Why you hung up on me the other night."

"I was in a hospital, too," Joanna said, sounding defensive.

"You were?" He stood up. Joanna noticed that it wasn't easy for him. He had always been so agile, so athletic. But now his legs seemed stiff. He seemed to move with real pain. "What happened to you?"

"When you fell, I — I ran for help."

It's the truth, Joanna thought. Why do I feel as if I'm lying?

"Yeah?"

"Yeah. I started driving to town to get the police, or an ambulance or something. But I — I was so upset, I got into an accident. I was unconscious for a day. But I guess I was lucky."

"We both were," Dex said with real emotion. "I've missed you a lot."

He hurried to her, leaned down, put his arms around her shoulders, and kissed her. Joanna kissed him back, suddenly feeling emotional, too.

He's real, all right, she thought. He's not a ghost.

The kiss lasted a long time. She grabbed the back of his head and held him to her.

What am I doing? she thought.

Shep's face flashed into her mind.

Pressing her lips against Dex's, holding his head, gripping his long hair, she felt terribly confused.

I *do* feel something for him, she thought.

Don't I?

Or am I just relieved that he's okay?

This isn't right. This isn't what I want.

So why am I doing it?

Again, Shep's face flashed into her mind.

She pulled back suddenly and dropped her hands to her side. He stayed there, leaning down over her, his dark eyes burning into hers.

"I really thought you were dead," she said.

"I'm not. I'll prove it," he said, and kissed her again.

Something's wrong, she thought. Something's different.

This kiss was much shorter. She heard noises, footsteps in the hall.

"My mom — she's up."

"Okay. I'd better go. I'll pick you up Friday night," he whispered. "I'll prove to you I'm not dead."

"Friday night?"

"Yeah." He kissed her again.

"But, Dex — "

She had to tell him about Shep. She didn't really want to go out with Dex.

But she did.

She was terribly confused.

He disappeared out the window. She listened to him slide down the tree.

Something is different about him, Joanna thought. His kiss. It felt different. Just not the same.

Trying to figure out what it was that was different, she fell into a troubled sleep.

Chapter 9

"Well, I'm sorry, Shep. I'm disappointed, too." Joanna blew on her nail polish, cradling the phone on her shoulder.

Shep whined on the other end.

She didn't mind the whining. She was pleased that her breaking their date had gotten him so upset.

"Well, what about tomorrow night? I'm sure the same movie will be playing tomorrow night."

Shep had to go somewhere with his parents tomorrow night.

"Well, maybe next week," Joanna said, glancing at the clock. She was supposed to meet Dex at the mall in five minutes.

Oh, well. Let Dex wait a while, she thought. It wouldn't be the first time. She thought of that night back in October when she had hidden behind a post and watched him wait. What a hoot!

Why won't these nails dry?

Now Shep was asking if he could stop by later. No way, dude.

"No, that's not a good idea, Shep. My mom is really sick. It's the flu. That's why I promised I'd stay home."

He wanted to talk more, but she hung up, careful not to smudge her nails. What a good liar I am, she thought. Even I believed that story. Dex thinks he's such a good actor. But I can act circles around him!

Dex.

Was she really going out with Dex?

More to the point: *Why* was she going out with Dex?

She really didn't feel anything for him anymore. She didn't like admitting it — even to herself — but she had felt that tiny little bit of disappointment upon learning that he was alive.

She tried to force that thought from her mind. It was an unspeakable thought, after all. But somehow it kept drifting to the surface of her thoughts.

So why *was* she standing up Shep so she could go to the movies with Dex tonight?

Frankly, she admitted, she didn't know. She felt very confused.

She was sure that after spending the evening with Dex, she'd be able to start sorting things out in her mind.

Shep was so sweet, so boyish, so charming. So right.

It had to be guilt. That was the only reason she was pulling on her best blue Ralph Lauren sweater over her designer jeans, giving her hair one more quick brush, and hurrying downstairs to get the car.

"Night, Mom," she called. "Don't wait up!"

What a laugh. Her mother had never cared enough to wait up, not once.

"You and Shep have a good time!" her mother called from the study.

"Right!" Joanna called back.

What she doesn't know won't hurt her. She doesn't even know that I thought Dex was dead. She doesn't have to know that I'm seeing him again.

She grabbed her big, expensive, fur-lined coat. She always felt so safe and protected inside it. She stepped into the garage from the house entrance. The light went on automatically. She slid behind the steering wheel of her mother's new BMW. The leather seat felt cold against her hand. The car started with a gentle hum, and she backed down the drive and headed to the mall.

Dex was pacing back and forth in front of the bookstore. *This is where I came in,* Joanna thought drily.

He looked so pale.

That was the first thing she noticed about him.

The high fluorescent lights made everyone else look yellow. But Dex's skin, Joanna immediately noticed, was white, nearly as white as cake flour.

He was wearing the same black jeans and leather bomber jacket. His black hair was brushed straight back and tied in a short ponytail. He was limping slightly as he paced, favoring his left leg.

She had the sudden urge to turn around and drive to Shep's house. She hadn't been looking forward to this date. In fact, she'd been dreading it, in a way. Dreading what they might talk about. Dreading what they couldn't talk about.

"Hi, Joanna!"

Too late. Dex had spotted her. A crooked smile crossed his face.

That's not his smile, she thought. His smile was always so straight, so open. That's not his smile at all. It's a stranger's smile.

Oh, just knock it off, she scolded herself. Stop looking for differences.

Of *course* Dex is different. He fell off a cliff, remember? He broke nearly every bone in his body. He was in a hospital for two months.

That could make you seem a little bit different.

"Hi, Dex. Sorry I'm late." She took his hand. It was ice cold.

"Cold hands," she said, startled. His hands were always so warm. He was always so warm. He'd walk around in his shirtsleeves in the coldest winter weather and never seemed to notice that everyone else was freezing.

"Oh. Sorry." He pulled his hand away with an apologetic smile. He seemed really nervous. "The movie just started. I'm sure we didn't miss much," he said, leading the way across the mall to the theater, limping as he walked.

The movie was some kind of action comedy with Robert DeNiro grinning and shooting a lot of people, and then driving a pickup truck the wrong way on a freeway with a dozen police cars chasing him.

Joanna couldn't concentrate on the movie. It seemed so strange to be sitting next to Dex, sitting so close to him in the dark again.

A few minutes into the film, he slid his arm around her shoulder. She leaned against him, her eyes on the screen.

What was that odor?

She sniffed once, twice, then stopped because Dex was beginning to notice.

It was a slightly musty smell, sour like old fruit. Or meat that had gone bad.

She turned her head away, but the stale odor followed her.

Dex had always smelled so sweet.

What was causing that sickening smell?

Chapter 10

"Dex is alive," Joanna said, unable to suppress a grin.

Mary's mouth dropped open. She turned positively pale. "No!" she cried when she could finally speak.

"Yes. He's alive. I went out with him last night."

Mary put her hands over her ears and shook her head, her tight, brown curls seeming to vibrate around her. "I don't think I'm hearing right, Joanna. Dex — ?"

"He's alive," Joanna repeated, enjoying her friend's shocked reaction.

It was Sunday afternoon. Mrs. Collier had gone out shopping again. Mary had dropped by unannounced, the first time Joanna had seen her since the hospital visit.

"But — but — Pete told me — "

"Me, too," Joanna interrupted. "What's Pete's problem, anyway?"

"I don't know. I haven't seen him," Mary replied,

still stunned. She flung herself back onto the crushed velvet sofa, rested her head against the back, and stared up at the elaborate crystal light fixture suspended from the ceiling. "Whew. Joanna. Really. Just let me catch my breath. What a shock."

"Tell me about it," Joanna said drily, tucking her legs beneath her on the big, overstuffed armchair. "He climbed in my bedroom window last week. Can you imagine?"

"At night?"

"At night. I was terrified. I thought I was seeing a ghost."

"But Dex is okay? Really?" The color still hadn't returned to her face.

"Yeah. Pretty much. He limps a little. I guess he was beat up pretty bad by the fall. He was in a hospital upstate for the past two months. But he seems perfectly okay now."

Except for the cold hands and the weird smell, Joanna added to herself. But what was the point of mentioning that to Mary?

"Wow," Mary said. She closed her eyes tightly. "Wow."

"I should call Pete and tell him that was a really rotten joke he pulled," Joanna said, more to herself than to Mary. "It's really the sickest thing I've ever heard. And I believed him."

"Of course. Me, too," Mary said, opening her eyes. "Why would he tell a stupid lie like that? It's so cruel. Pete's a pretty strange guy, but I never thought he was cruel."

"I never liked him," Joanna confessed. "I only put up with him because of Dex."

"And you really went out with Dex?"

"Yeah. Last night. I had to break a date with Shep to do it."

"Shep?"

"Yeah. You remember Shep. Blond hair. Really tall. Has a great smile. And a Jaguar." Joanna laughed.

Mary was thinking too hard to laugh. "Dex is really alive? How come he never called you?"

Joanna shrugged. "He was beat up too bad. He asked his aunt to try, but you know how flipped-out she is. She probably doesn't remember how to use a phone. Besides, I was in the hospital for over a month, too. Dex didn't know that."

"And you're going with Shep now?"

Joanna nodded.

"Well, are you going to tell him about Dex?"

"No. What for? I think I can string them both along for a while."

"Won't Shep get suspicious when — "

"Shep is so crazy about me, he'll put up with anything I do," Joanna said. She realized it sounded a bit boastful, but it was the truth.

Mary made a disapproving face.

"Don't look at me like that," Joanna said, only half teasing.

"You're awful," Mary muttered. She was only half teasing, too.

The two girls stared at each other without any

real warmth. Joanna realized that she couldn't be as close to Mary as she had been. They had obviously grown apart.

It's not my fault, Joanna told herself. Mary's just changed. What right does she have to sit on my couch like that and judge me?

"Well, how do you feel about it?" Mary asked, still struggling to understand. "Do you still like Dex?"

Joanna yawned. The conversation was becoming tiresome to her. She had enjoyed shocking Mary with the news and watching the stunned expression on her face. But now she wished Mary would go home.

"I don't really know if I like Dex or not," she said flatly. It was kind of fun trying to shock Mary with her coldness.

"Huh?"

"I don't think I like him anymore. I mean, as a boyfriend. I guess I just . . . feel guilty."

"Guilty? What do you mean? Because you thought he was dead, and he wasn't?" Mary pulled herself up straight and leaned forward, her hands on the knees of her faded jeans.

Joanna realized that Mary didn't really know the details of that night. She didn't know that Joanna hadn't stayed to help rescue Dex. That Joanna had driven off without seeing if Dex was dead or alive.

"I mean, I feel guilty because I'm the one who drove him to the Promontory that night. He wouldn't have fallen if he hadn't been showing off for me."

"Oh. I see." Mary seemed disappointed by Joanna's answer.

What does she want from me? Joanna asked herself.

She decided to change the subject. "Let's talk about *you* for a while, Mary. What's new in your life?"

Mary sighed and flopped back against the couch. "Nothing compared to you," she said. "I'm sorry, Joanna, but I just can't believe that Dex is alive. It's like — like a miracle! And you're being so calm about it."

So cold, she means, Joanna thought. "So are you going out with anyone?" she asked, running her hands back through her short blonde hair.

Mary shook her head. "No. My life is as boring as ever. I had my hair highlighted last week. See?" She lowered her head so Joanna could see the blonde streaks among the dark curls. Joanna hadn't noticed the change. "That's about the most interesting thing that's happened to me."

Joanna laughed, but quickly cut it off, realizing it wasn't an appropriate response. Mary was really feeling sorry for herself. Joanna just wasn't in the mood to cluck sympathetically and say, "There, there."

She was grateful when the ringing telephone interrupted their conversation.

"Hello. Dex? Hi." She gave Mary a meaningful look.

"Let me talk to him," Mary said. She leaped off the couch and grabbed the phone from Joanna's hand. "Dex? Is it really you? It's me, Mary."

Mary's dark eyes were wide with excitement. She was breathing heavily.

"I — I can't hear you very well," she said, frowning. "You sound so faint. Like you're very far away."

Dex said something. Mary obviously had to struggle to hear him. Joanna wished she'd give back the phone.

"Dex — I'm so happy!" Mary gushed. "I'm just so glad you're okay. Pete told us — well . . . never mind. I'm just so glad! I can't wait to see you sometime. Here. I'll give you back to Joanna."

She handed the phone to Joanna. "He sounds weird," she said. "Very far away."

"It's just a bad connection," Joanna said, raising the receiver to her ear. "Hi, Dex. What? You'll have to speak up. There's a lot of static or something."

He continued to talk quietly. It was as if he couldn't raise his voice. He asked her out for Friday night. "Yeah. I guess," she said, thinking of Shep. They chatted a few minutes more, but she really couldn't hear him. It wasn't just the background static. It was also the fact that his voice sounded weak and thin. Tired.

When she hung up, Mary was pulling on her blue down jacket. "Guess I'd better be going."

"I'm so glad you stopped by," Joanna said, putting on a sincere smile, then adding, "stranger."

Mary stopped at the door, and turned back with

a concerned look on her face. "You know, Dex's been through so much. You should be fair with him, don't you think? You really should tell him about Shep."

Joanna shrugged. "It's too interesting this way," she said, holding the door open for her friend. "I think I'll just play it out and see what happens."

Chapter 11

Joanna swung easily and the ball sailed over the net.

"Perfect," Rod, her instructor, said, flashing all 320 zillion perfect, sparkling white teeth. "Placement. Placement."

What does *that* mean? Joanna asked herself, shaking her head.

I'm going to have to say bye-bye to you, Rod, if you keep up that "placement" nonsense. She had the sneaking suspicion that she could probably beat him in a real game.

"Pick a spot, then place it there," he said, wiping his tanned forehead with a white handkerchief.

I haven't worked up a sweat. What's *his* problem? Joanna thought. "Hey, can I work on my backhand a while?" she called. She was paying for it. Why couldn't she work on what she *wanted* to work on?

"Okay, sure." He stuffed the handkerchief back into the pocket of his tennis shorts. "I'll hit a few to your left. Let's see your backhand. Try to smooth it out today, okay?"

Smooth it out?

What did *that* mean?

Was she losing her mind, or was Rod just an inane idiot?

This was definitely the last day for Mr. Smile Face. He hadn't given her a single pointer she could use. At sixty-five dollars an hour — plus tip — she expected a little more than "smooth it out."

He tapped the ball to the left. She jogged easily and smacked it back, using her backhand. She loved the *ping* the ball made on contact with the racquet. It was her favorite part of tennis. That little *ping*. So satisfying, somehow. She could hear dozens of *pings* all around her, as people played or took lessons on the vast indoor courts of the private tennis club.

Look at that fatso over there, wearing a parachute for tennis shorts, she thought, snickering at the woman chasing a ball across the next court. If I looked like that, I wouldn't play tennis. I'd shoot myself instead.

Another high bouncer from Rod. She reached back and returned it easily.

"Smooth. Very smooth. Nice follow-through," he called.

"Thanks a bunch."

"Time out. I've got to collect some more balls," he said, running across the court to get the ball basket.

Joanna sighed and lowered her racquet. She looked down the row of courts. A guy down at the end court looked a little like Shep. Not quite as good-looking.

She thought about Shep. He had come over Sunday night and they had gone for a long drive in his Jag. It was a clear, cold night. He had wanted to park up at the Promontory. She had hesitated at first and started to make an excuse. That was a place she never wanted to visit again.

But then she decided, what the heck.

It was just a place, after all. Just a rock cliff.

Just a makeout spot.

Just a place to get close to Shep.

She could probably push what had happened there out of her mind. It had been months ago, anyway.

What the heck.

And to her surprise, being back on that high cliff overlooking the town, being back on the very spot where the rock had crumbled and Dex had fallen, wasn't disturbing to her at all.

Dex had lived, after all.

Dex was okay.

Everyone was okay. So why should she feel funny about being back there?

It was so warm and cozy in the Jaguar with Shep. The windows all fogged over, and they were in their own world, their own little cocoon. Not on the Promontory. Not in the boring, little town of Middlewood. But locked away in their own tiny space capsule, just the two of them, so close, so close.

When that carful of teenagers drove up behind them with their brights on and the radio blaring, laughing and honking the horn, Joanna just wanted to kill them.

What right did they have to bring her back down to earth?

Sighing, she looked back to the tennis club waiting area. Shep was supposed to pick her up after her tennis lesson. Maybe he was early.

When she saw Dex back there behind the mesh wall, she uttered a low cry of surprise.

Dex?

What on earth is *he* doing here?

He was pacing back and forth behind the wire-mesh wall that separated the courts from the spectator area. Why was he walking so stiffly? His limp seemed to have gotten much more pronounced. Both legs appeared stiff now.

She raised her racquet over her head, trying to get his attention. Then she quickly lowered it.

His skin.

What on earth was wrong with his skin?

He looked positively green.

Maybe it's just the lights, Joanna thought. But there were other people watching the matches from behind the mesh wall, and their skin looked perfectly normal.

With that stiff-legged walk and the greenish skin, he looks just like Frankenstein, Joanna thought.

"Hey, Joanna — "

She realized Rod was calling to her. But she couldn't take her eyes off Dex. Was he sick or something?

"Hey, Joanna — ". How long had Rod been calling? "Don't lose your concentration. Come on!"

"I'm ready," she said, turning back to face the net. But she couldn't get the sight of Dex out of her mind, the green face, the pained, straight-legged walk.

"Remember your follow-through," Rod said, lobbing a ball over the net.

She had to run for this one. "Darn!" She was off-stride and the ball hit the edge of the racquet and bounced into the next court. "Sorry."

Rod sent one into the back court. This time she got there in time and, using her backhand, sent it sailing over his head.

"Out!" he cried.

Oh, who cares? she thought.

She turned back. Dex was gone.

Maybe it wasn't Dex, she thought. Why would Dex be here, anyway? He doesn't know I have a tennis lesson this afternoon. And why would he be all the way over on this side of town on a school day?

"Time's up," Rod said, smiling, twirling his racquet in his hand. He walked around the net and joined her on her side of the court. "Good workout?"

"Yeah. Fine," Joanna said without enthusiasm. She turned around again, searched the waiting area. No Dex.

"I like your racquet," Rod said. "I was going to buy that one, but I couldn't afford it."

"Yeah. It's good," Joanna said, looking down at the racquet. "See you next time." She started toward the locker room.

"Okay. Good backhand," Rod called after her. "We'll work on it more next time."

She didn't reply, just kept jogging off the courts. Maybe he isn't such a bad instructor, she thought. I mean, a tennis instructor doesn't exactly have to be a genius.

She showered quickly and changed back into her school clothes, carefully folding her tennis shorts and T-shirt into the canvas bag she had brought. Shep was waiting at the door. "How'd you do?" he asked, giving her a warm smile and carrying the bag for her.

It was a cold, sunny day. She zipped up her down jacket. "Fine. The instructor is a real jerk. But I got in some practice on my backhand." She followed him across the street to his car.

"I can't wait to get you on the court at the country club this spring," Shep said, tossing her bag in the back, then sliding into the driver's seat. "I'll give your backhand a workout."

"Are you any good?" Joanna asked.

"No," he replied. "Not very. Just good enough to be all-state my sophomore year."

"Big deal," she said. She started to make a joke, but her breath caught in her throat.

Dex.

It really was Dex. He was standing close enough to be seen clearly now.

He was leaning against the brick wall in the half-empty parking lot beside the tennis club, his hands shoved into his jeans pockets. Even in the sunlight, his skin looked green.

Almost reptilian, Joanna thought queasily.

Dex had been looking at the ground, but now he looked up and directed his stare at them.

Does he see us? Joanna wondered.

He must. He's looking right at me.

Shep reached into his pocket for the car keys, dropped them on the floor.

Joanna stared across the street at Dex.

Dex's eyes caught hers. They suddenly seemed to glow ruby-red, like the red eyes in a bad flash photo. Glowing red eyes like a dog's eyes at night.

Chapter 12

"So tell me again," Shep said, standing very close to her at the entrance to their school, making Joanna back up till she bumped into the coat closet door. "Why can't you go out with me both Friday and Saturday night?"

She gave him a playful little shove to give herself breathing room. A couple of girls she knew giggled as they passed by in the fast-emptying corridor. "I have to get home," she said, trying to avoid the question. "Why are you pushing me into the coat room?"

He grinned and took a big step forward, forcing her further back. "Just answer the question."

"Really, Shep. You're being a pig."

"Oink. Oink."

Joanna hated it when he tried to be playful. It just wasn't the right style for him, she thought. She liked him much better when he was serious and quiet and played it straight.

"I already explained it to you," she said wearily, shoving him again, a little harder this time, then dashing out into the middle of the hall so he couldn't back her up again.

"Hello, Mr. Munroe," they both said, as their French teacher passed by, probably on his way to the teachers' lounge. The paunchy, middle-aged teacher nodded and smiled and kept walking.

"I have to study Friday night," Joanna lied. "I missed so much school because of the accident, Mom insists that I spend one weekend night studying. That's the whole reason, Shep. So stop being insulted."

Was he buying that story?

Yes. He seemed to be.

"Well, fine," he said, kicking at the wall plaster down by the linoleum floor with the toe of his brown Frye boot. "So why don't I come over Friday night, and we'll study together?"

"No way," she said, her grin mirroring the devilish grin on his face. "If you came over, we wouldn't study, and you know it."

"We could study," he said. "Really."

"No. Really," she insisted. "No way. At least not this weekend, okay?"

"Well. . . ."

She loved how disappointed he looked.

"I'm really serious," she said. "I want to graduate on time. I don't want to have to do an extra semester because of that stupid car accident. I *have* to catch up with the work. Understand?"

"Of course I do," he said, brightening a little. "Of course."

She looked both ways to make sure no one was

in the corridor, then kissed him quickly on the cheek. "Thanks," she whispered.

I love the fact that he's so gullible, so trusting, Joanna thought, pulling on her jacket. I'm also glad that Dex lives way on the other side of town. It makes it so much easier to keep Shep and Dex from knowing about each other.

She realized she'd have to break up with Dex soon. She didn't really care about him at all. But he was useful. It was kind of fun to keep Shep guessing, to make him uncomfortable. And the idea of having two boyfriends at once really appealed to Joanna. It was a lot like having two winter coats, she told herself. It was nice to be able to trade them off.

Friday night she drove across town to meet Dex. He slid into the car, holding something carefully out of sight. Suddenly he reached for her, and something silver glinted in his hand. "Dex!" gasped Joanne, jumping. The car swerved.

"Surprise," said Dex, pinning a corsage to the shoulder of her coat. "Oh," said Joanne. "How nice."

They went to a small dance club in his neighborhood. "Why is it called Barks?" Joanna asked, carefully locking the BMW.

"You'll see," Dex said, climbing stiffly out of the car.

Once inside, the reason for the club's name became obvious. There were giant dogs painted on all the walls. "This place is really tacky," Joanna said, shaking her head as she surveyed the awful dog paintings and then the small dance floor with its flashing strobe light.

"And what is that awful moose head doing on the wall?" she asked. "Mooses don't bark!"

"I knew you'd like this place," Dex said, laughing.

His cheeks seemed to sag when he laughed, Joanna noticed.

He looks so different, she thought.

"The sound system is good," he said, leading her onto the dance floor. "And it doesn't get too crowded."

There were six or seven couples on the floor, dancing to a slow, rhythmic Gloria Estefan record. Joanna looked across the dance floor at a particularly ugly wall painting of a German shepherd rearing up on its hind legs with its head tilted back in a howl.

"Come on, let's dance," she said, shouting over the music. "It's better than staring at these paintings."

He took her hand. Again, his hand was ice cold. He smiled at her, his old, familiar smile. But it seemed somehow lifeless, as if it were a real struggle for him to smile.

He seems so different, she thought, as they started to dance, bumping into other couples until they found a space for themselves on the small rectangular floor. He was always so lively, so theatrical, so excited about everything all the time.

Now he was dancing half-heartedly with her, almost moving in slow motion, hardly moving his feet at all.

The rhythm slowed. It became a tuneful song with a slow salsa beat.

He moved closer to her, holding her with his cold hands.

That smell again.

That musty odor.

The odor of decay.

"Dex — are you wearing cologne or something?"

"What?" He struggled to hear her over the deafening sound system.

"Are you wearing cologne?" she repeated, shouting right by his ear.

He made a face. "Of course not."

He laughed, an unpleasant laugh.

I've never heard that laugh before, Joanna thought, staring into his face.

He's like a stranger, she thought. He's just so different.

Then suddenly he stopped dancing and held his hand up to his mouth.

"Dex — what's the matter?"

He didn't reply. Maybe he didn't hear her over the blaring music.

He seemed to flicker on and off under the flashing strobe light. One second he was bright and colorful in the maroon shirt he wore over his faded jeans. The next second he was shrouded in darkness, a dark figure holding his mouth, walking stiffly off the dance floor.

"Dex?"

She followed him. "Hey — wait up. What's the matter?"

He bumped into a girl in a woolly white sweater

and short red skirt and just kept going. The girl turned around angrily, surprised by his rudeness.

Joanna wasn't sure whether Dex wanted her to follow him or not. It was as if he'd forgotten about her.

He stopped in front of a floor-to-ceiling mirror against the back wall and peered into it as he fiddled with something in his mouth.

Reluctantly she came up behind him. "Dex — what's the matter?"

"Oh nothing," he said, removing his fingers from his mouth. He turned to face her, looking embarrassed.

"Nothing?"

"Loose teeth. That's all."

She laughed, then realized it wasn't funny. "Aren't you a little old to still be losing your teeth?"

He stared at her coldly. "It's just loose," he said. "It'll be okay."

She suddenly realized that it must have been caused by his fall off the cliff. He'd never wanted to talk about the injuries he had gotten from the fall. And, of course, neither did she.

She assumed that he was beat up pretty badly, but that he was basically okay now. But the fact that he suddenly had a loose tooth made her wonder.

"Dex — your legs. You've been limping. Is it because — "

"They'll be okay," he said quickly, not letting her finish.

He suddenly looked very tired.

They stared at each other awkwardly. "My legs are all right," he said finally. "I guess I'm doing a lot better than I ever expected." He laughed for some reason, a bitter laugh.

"You've got to get some sun," she said, touching his shoulder. "You look positively green."

He shrugged. "Maybe I'll charter a private jet and fly to the Bahamas."

"Hey, Dex — that's not your kind of joke. That's *my* kind of joke." ·

"You and your mother take a winter vacation every year," he said thoughtfully, ignoring her remark. "Maybe you'd like to take me along this year." He reached up and played with his loose tooth, turning back to the mirror.

What a thought! Joanna nearly laughed out loud. She could just picture her mother's reaction if Joanna asked to bring Dex along to St. Croix.

What a thought!

She was sorry she had said anything about his looking so green. She was sorry she had brought up his appearance at all.

She was sorry she had gone out with him.

He used to be so exciting, she thought bitterly, watching him in the mirror as he fiddled with the loose tooth.

"Want to dance some more?" she asked, trying to get him away from the mirror and end their conversation at the same time. "That's why we came here, right?"

He turned around slowly. "Let's get a Coke or something first, okay?"

"Yeah. Sure. Why don't you do that? I'll wait over by that table for you."

He nodded agreement and, walking stiff-legged, practically dragging his left leg after him, he headed toward the bar on the other side of the dance floor.

He really does look green, she thought.

I think he was more badly injured in the fall than he's letting on to me.

I think his knees are really damaged.

And his face. . . .

Suddenly he stopped at the edge of the dance floor.

What's his problem? Joanna wondered, staring across the room at him. Why did he stop there?

"Oh good lord — no!"

She didn't realize she had screamed out loud.

Her breath caught in her throat. She suddenly felt sick.

She was sure she had just seen Dex reach up and pull a big chunk of skin off his face.

Chapter 13

"You look wonderful, Joanna. Stand up straight."

"Mom, I *am* standing up straight."

"Well, maybe it's the dress then."

"Mom — just stop it," Joanna cried. "You're just trying to make me feel self-conscious."

Mrs. Collier's mouth dropped open. "Me? Why on *earth* would I do that?"

Because you know you look like a frumpy little mouse in that dreadful evening dress you're wearing, and you want me to feel as bad as you look, Joanna thought. But she decided not to reply at all.

She walked side by side with her mother up the concrete steps of the old armory and into the brightly lit Main Hall. "Ugh! Those hideous portraits!" The walls were filled with gigantic, dark paintings of nineteenth-century town founders and other dignitaries.

"Joanna — please. Don't be so negative."

"What a place for a party," Joanna said, slipping

off her coat and handing it to the young man behind the coat check counter.

"You just have to be nice and charming for a few hours," her mother said, fussing with her enormous fur coat. She couldn't manage to unbutton the top button. Joanna finally did it for her. "That's all I'm asking. It isn't that hard, is it?"

Joanna looked glumly around the drafty old hall. "I'll do my best, Mom."

Every year the Ladies Club had their winter charity drive here in the armory. This year, her mother had volunteered to be chairwoman of the event.

Why not? Joanna had thought. She has nothing better to do.

But then Mrs. Collier roped Joanna into coming to the affair and helping serve at the punch table.

It was going to be an endless night, Joanna knew, even though it was supposed to end at eleven. She had done everything she could to get out of it, even faking the stomach flu. But her mother wasn't buying any excuse.

An entire Saturday night wasted, she moaned to herself, adjusting the straps of her green velvet dress and making her way over to the gigantic crystal punch bowl on the table by the wall.

I could be out with Shep. Or Dex.

She hadn't seen Dex for over a week, not since that unpleasant night at that dreadful dance club. He had called a couple of times during the week and had actually sounded very pleasant, a bit more like his old self.

She and Shep had gone to a movie the night before, a very funny Tom Hanks comedy. Shep had laughed like a lunatic. She had never seen him let go like that. He had a ridiculous laugh, she decided. She actually liked him a lot better when he was serious. But she was glad to see him loosen up like that. They had a really nice night.

And now here she was in the armory, of all places. Staring up at the dour, bewhiskered face of William Beathard Rogerson, 1849–1910. Why did he pose with his hand in his shirt like that? Joanna wondered. Did he have an itch?

The hall filled quickly, mostly with old and middle-aged people in furs and formal evening wear. Joanna sighed wistfully. Is this *me* in forty years? she asked herself.

No way, José.

She plastered a smile on her face and, thinking about Dex, wondering what he was doing tonight, she started to serve punch in the crystal cups stacked beside the punch bowl.

"Aren't you Dorothy's daughter?" asked a woman in a violet strapless gown.

"Yes, I am," Joanna said through her plastered-on smile. "Would you like some punch?"

The woman was wearing purple lipstick that matched her dress. Her face was heavily rouged. She had wavy, silver hair, very stylishly short. "Certainly, dear. Your mother tells me that you're dating Shephard Forrest."

Joanna, startled, spilled a little punch over the side of the cup. "Yes, I am." What was her mother doing — broadcasting it to the whole town?

"Well, I've known his family for years," the woman said, reaching out a violet-gloved hand to shake Joanna's free hand. "I'm Sylvia Norris."

"How do you do, Mrs. Norris." Joanna handed her the cup of punch.

"He's a fine young man, and you're a perfect couple."

"Thank you."

Luckily a white-haired gentleman in a satiny black tuxedo tapped Mrs. Norris on the shoulder. She turned to greet him and they strolled off together chattering enthusiastically.

She's actually very well preserved for her age, Joanna thought. I hope I can still wear purple lipstick when I'm a doddering old geezer.

And she's right about Shep and me. We *are* a perfect couple.

So why do I keep going out with Dex?

It's crazy.

It's just not like me.

She poured out two cups of punch and placed them in waiting hands.

It's obviously a character flaw, she told herself.

That's what it is. Dex is just a flaw in my character.

I'm going to say good-bye to him next weekend. Maybe I should just write him a letter.

No. He would never believe it in a letter. The next thing I'd know he'd be climbing into my bedroom in the middle of the night, saying let's go for a ride, or something crazy, pretending he never even received it.

No. I have to break up with him in person. Face to face.

She pictured Dex's face. He used to be so good-looking.

She pictured his green complexion.

Then she saw the chunk of skin drop off.

That didn't really happen — did it?

Of course, she had imagined it. But why was he so different? Why did he act and look so different?

It's all over between him and me, she thought, pouring more punch, smiling like a robot at two plump, well-dressed women who returned the robot-smile.

That's it. I'm breaking up with him next Saturday night.

I don't care if he did almost die that night on the Promontory. That was his own stupid idea. The whole thing was his fault. Going there in the first place. Showing off like a fool on the cliff edge. Falling.

I don't feel guilty anymore. I just don't.

I don't feel anything. And I can't keep seeing him week after week, pretending that I still care about him because of that one stupid night.

Having made the decision, she banished Dex from her mind. She concentrated on thinking about Shep for the rest of the evening. He was so good-looking. So nice. So right for her.

She decided she even liked his silly laugh.

At about eleven-fifteen, Joanna's mother, looking flushed and excited after the successful evening, told Joanna to take the car and go home. "I'm going out with the Waynes and the Sturbridges," she said, squeezing Joanna's arm. "They'll drop me home later. Thanks for helping out, dear."

"Thanks for forcing me," Joanna said, and laughed so her mother would know it was a joke.

A few minutes later, she had wrapped her coat around her and hurried down the armory stairs to the parking lot. She started to hand the parking ticket to the attendant, and then stopped in surprise.

"Pete!"

It took him a little while to recognize her, probably because he had never seen her so dressed up. "Joanna?"

"How are you? I mean, what are you doing here?" she sputtered. He looked exactly the same, same bad skin, same spiky hair.

"I'm . . . uh . . . parking cars," he said somewhat defensively. "The pay is really good. And I get overtime for Saturday nights."

"Hey, that's great," she said with false enthusiasm. They stared at each other. She still had the parking ticket in her hand.

"So how've you been? I haven't seen you in so long," she said, wishing she could get her car and get out of there without having to make small talk with Pete.

"Yeah. It's been a while," he said, slapping his hands together, probably to keep them warm. He frowned.

"Listen, I've been seeing Dex," Joanna said, fumbling for something to say. "I'm surprised he hasn't mentioned you. He — "

Pete's face filled with confusion. "You *what*?"

"I've been seeing Dex. Something's wrong with him, don't you think? He looks so — "

"Joanna — what are you talking about?" He shook his head, a strange grin on his face. "You're putting me on, right?"

"Putting you on?"

"Yeah. That's a real bad joke, you know." He kicked at the curb.

"Pete, I saw Dex last week and — "

"Have you totally flipped out? Dex is dead. He's dead, Joanna."

"Pete, stop. He isn't dead. Why do you keep telling me that? I saw him last week. I touched him. I danced with him. He's not dead. Why do you insist on — "

"I don't get what you're trying to pull. Are you crazy, or what?" Pete glared at her angrily, searching her eyes as if trying to discover whether or not she was serious. "I only know one thing, Joanna," he said in a low voice she had to struggle to hear. "Dex is dead."

"But — "

"I went to his funeral. I saw him in the box. He was dead. Stone-cold dead."

"Pete — "

"Maybe you *think* you see Dex," Pete continued heatedly. "Maybe you imagine it out of guilt or something. I mean, you *should* feel guilty, you know. You left him there to die."

"I did not! I — " Oh, what's the use of trying to explain? she thought.

"Maybe you need some kind of help or something. I'm no shrink. Like I said, I only know one thing. Dex is dead. He's dead, Joanna. I saw him die. And I saw him at his funeral. He's dead. Forever. And that's the truth."

Chapter 14

Joanna drove home slowly, carefully, her mind spinning from her conversation with Pete. She gripped the wheel to stop from shaking. Even though she turned the heater up full force, she couldn't get warm.

She was still trembling when she climbed out of the car and entered the house through the garage. She changed into warm, comfortable clothes, a heavy wool sweater and soft, blue running pants. Then she made herself a cup of tea. But she still couldn't get calm, couldn't stop hearing Pete's frightening words.

I believe Pete, she decided.

But how *could* she believe Pete?

What did that mean? If she believed Pete, that meant she'd been dating a *ghost*.

And Dex was no ghost. She was sure of that.

"It doesn't make sense!" she screamed aloud, immediately regretting it because she didn't want to wake the maid.

She carried her tea from the kitchen into the living room, and turned on all the lights. The tea warmed her a bit. The trembling stopped.

There has to be a logical explanation for this.

There's a logical explanation for everything, right?

She sat down on the big, overstuffed armchair, curled her feet under her, and placed the mug of tea in her lap.

Let's just think about this. . . .

But there was no way to think about it logically.

Dex was dead. Pete had told her that back in October in the hospital. Then in December, just a few weeks ago, Dex reappeared. He had been hurt, he said. And he looked and acted as if he'd been hurt. But he was alive. He was definitely alive.

Except for the fact that Pete insisted he was dead. And Pete had been at the funeral.

So that meant . . .

That meant . . .

What?

When Mrs. Collier returned home shortly after one, Joanna was still sitting in the armchair in the living room, still staring at the wallpaper, the now empty tea mug in her hand.

"Good heavens, Joanna. I thought you'd be asleep."

"Well, no, I — "

"What a night!" her mother gushed. "And what a smashing success. Do you know how much money we raised for the charity fund?"

"No." Joanna didn't pretend to be interested.

"It was a lot. Do you know what Mrs. Norris said to me? She said . . ."

Her mother rattled on. Joanna tuned her out. Her voice became a quiet hum in the background of Joanna's thoughts. She nodded occasionally and said "Uh-huh" to make her mother think she was listening. She could go on like this for half an hour without taking a breath, Joanna thought. Well, let her. This is the highlight of her year, after all. Poor thing.

Joanna thought about Dex, trying to arrange the puzzle pieces of this mystery together. But the pieces just wouldn't fit.

Dex, even though he seemed different, was definitely Dex.

She thought about how he had changed. The green tinge of his skin. The stiff, straight-legged walk, the musty, stale odor, the loose tooth, the skin that peeled off like . . . like a zombie.

Night of the Living Dead.

Yuck.

She scolded herself for getting carried away. Now think logically.

Zombies aren't logical.

"I don't think you've heard a word I said." Her mother stood up and headed to the front stairway.

"Of course I did. I heard every word," Joanna lied. "Listen, Mom, I've got to go out."

Mrs. Collier looked at her diamond-encrusted watch. "At this hour? Are you crazy?"

I *hope* I'm not crazy, Joanna thought.

"Uh . . . I'm just so wound up. From the party and all. You know. All the excitement. I can't seem to relax. I'm just going to take a short drive, just to get some fresh air."

"A drive? No, Joanna. Don't go driving late at night," her mother pleaded, wetting her finger and wiping something off the watch crystal. "Last time you went for a drive late at night, you — "

"I'll be careful, Mom." Thanks for pretending you care. "And I'll be back real soon. Promise."

Joanna hurried past her mother at the stairway, pulled her down coat from the coat closet, and headed to the garage. "Be careful!" her mother called after her. "I really don't approve of this!"

I don't approve, either, Joanna thought, backing the BMW down the drive. I'd much rather be tucked safely into my nice, warm bed.

But I've got to know the truth. I've got to know what's going on here.

As she turned onto Fairview, the street that would take her across town to Dex's house, a feeling of dread began to form in her stomach.

She suddenly had the feeling that knowing the truth might be even more frightening than *not* knowing.

Chapter 15

Dex's neighborhood was so much more squalid than she'd remembered. The houses were so claptrap, so small. They huddled together like little tents, one right after the other with hardly any front yard at all.

No wonder Dex always wants to meet on my side of town, Joanna thought, pushing the automatic lock button on the car door.

She slowed down as she neared his block. Across the narrow street, two scrawny dogs, looking like skeletons in her bright headlights, tipped over a garbage can. The lid clattered against the pavement and rolled into the center of the street. The mangy dogs began pulling at a large package wrapped in brown paper, each snarling at the other to let go.

Joanna swerved to miss the garbage can lid. The bony dogs were in her rearview mirror now. Even with the windows shut tight, she could hear their snarls and growls as they struggled to pull open the disgusting package.

Why do these people keep their garbage cans out on the street? Joanna wondered, holding her breath as if trying not to smell the garbage. And don't they ever feed their dogs?

Was that Dex's house up there? The small brick house with the newspaper stuffed in a broken window?

Yes, that was it. She'd been here once before.

Joanna slowed to a stop, but kept the car's engine running. The house was dark except for a single, low-watt bulb aglow over the narrow front stoop. An old tire sat in the middle of the small square patch that served as a front lawn. The yard seemed to be all weeds, weeds that hadn't been cut in months, bending first this way, then that in the shifting night wind.

Do I really know someone who lives *here*? Joanna thought.

How could I be going out with someone who has a tire in his front yard and newspaper stuffed in a window?

And what am I doing here now? The house is dark. He and his aunt are probably asleep.

This is crazy. Totally crazy.

She glanced down at the clock on the dashboard. One-thirty.

Dex usually stays up till all hours, she thought, staring up at the dark house. Maybe he isn't asleep. I drove all the way over here. I have to talk to him.

If I knock on the front door, his old aunt probably won't hear it anyway, and he'll come to the door.

Having made up her mind, she pulled the car to the curb. There was no driveway. She'd have to park on the street. She cut the headlights. The sudden darkness surprised her.

Can't they even afford streetlights? she asked herself.

Oh, well. When I break it off with Dex, I'll never have to come to this awful neighborhood again — unless it's part of some door-to-door charity drive.

Reluctantly she opened the car door and stepped out into the darkness. The wind was cold and strong. It seemed to push her away from the car. She pushed back, still clinging to the door handle.

This is a mistake. A stupid mistake.

No. I have to know the truth about Dex. I have to know — what?

If he's dead or alive?

The street was silent except for the wind. A narrow concrete walk, overgrown with weeds, led up to Dex's front stoop. Low shadows clustered against the front of the house like hunkering animals, caught in the dim yellow light of the bulb suspended over the door.

Joanna's footsteps sounded so loud as she walked quickly to the front door. Down the street another garbage can lid clattered against pavement, startling her. She gasped. The two dogs were barking in the distance, fighting over the garbage.

The smell of garbage floated around her, carried by the wind. She held her breath and stepped onto the front stoop.

For some reason she thought of the sweet smell, the smell Dex used to have whenever he held her close.

He didn't smell like that anymore. He smelled just like the garbage in the air.

She looked for a doorbell, but there wasn't one. The screen door, she saw, was torn at the top, one corner hanging down.

She took a deep breath and knocked gently on the door.

Dex — be awake.

Be awake, Dex.

Answer the door. And . . . be alive.

Tell me that Pete's a liar. Tell me that Pete has lost his mind. That Pete's been locked away in a looney bin. That he escaped and came to the armory just to scare me, just to make me as crazy as he is.

I always hated Pete.

With that stupid diamond stud in his ear and his hair standing straight up, moussed and sprayed so carefully. He's so disgusting and stupid.

I never understood why you liked him so much, Dex. I never understood what you two talked about, what you two were always laughing about.

Pete's such a stupid, typical jerk.

The wind gusted, pulling open the screen door.

Joanna, startled, uttered a low cry, and raised her hands to stop the door from swinging out and hitting her.

It was as if a ghost had pushed open the door, she thought.

Then she scolded herself for getting carried away.

Don't lose it totally, Joanna, she told herself. She knocked on the door, harder this time.

She listened. No sounds inside the house.

Maybe Dex isn't even home. It would be like him to be out till all hours.

Maybe I made this whole trip for nothing.

But what choice did I have? Pete got me so upset, I —

She knocked again, pounding the door with her fist.

Ouch. That hurt.

Still no sounds inside.

Okay. I tried.

She felt disappointed — and relieved.

She started to back off the stoop, still listening for signs of life inside — and bumped into someone.

Felt hot breath on the back of her neck.

Felt a hand on her shoulder.

Her scream seemed to be stifled by the wind. The sound caught in her throat.

She screamed again.

She couldn't help it.

And spun around to look into Dex's face.

"Dex?"

His dark eyes stared into hers, unblinking. His face revealed no emotion, no surprise at seeing her there, no excitement, no delight by her unexpected visit.

No emotion at all.

"Dex? Are you okay?"

He didn't reply.

"Sorry I screamed like that." She suddenly felt embarrassed. She had screamed like a little girl. That wasn't like her at all. "But you scared me. I wasn't expecting — "

He stepped into the dim light.

"Oh."

She couldn't hold in her cry of surprise.

He looked so terrible.

His skin was pea-soup green. His eyes, still not blinking, were red.

Joanna stared into his face, feeling the fear sweep through her, feeling the terror overwhelm her, freeze her there, hold her like the casts she had worn in the hospital.

His skin was peeling. His forehead was pocked and cratered, as if pieces of skin had fallen off.

His black hair, once so beautiful, so silky and beautiful, looked as if it had slipped to one side. The skin was missing from his scalp and a patch of gray showed through from underneath.

His *skull*?!

"Dex!" she cried, unable to stop staring even though she wanted to look away, to turn away — to run away. "Dex — are you all right?"

The smell. The horrible garbage smell.

It wasn't in the air.

It was coming from Dex.

It wasn't garbage, she thought, feeling sick. It was decay.

111

"Dex — why aren't you saying anything?"

He stared, unblinking.

"Dex — *please*! You're really *frightening* me!"

Finally he smiled.

The grin formed slowly, almost in slow motion.

I'm in a dream, Joanna suddenly thought. A slow motion dream.

Wake up, wake up, wake up.

As the grin formed, Dex's mouth opened.

"No!" Joanna screamed as she realized that his front teeth were gone.

He stepped forward, pressing her back against the torn screen door. He raised his hand. He was holding a corsage, a faded, tattered corsage, stabbed by a long, silver pin. Something dark dripped down the petals. He smelled like rotting meat. He grinned at her, his toothless grin.

"How about a kiss, Joanna?" he asked, his voice nothing but wind.

Chapter 16

"Joanna — what's wrong? Why aren't you getting dressed?"

"I — I can't." Joanna lifted her head from the pillow with a groan. "I think I'm sick."

Her mother, already dressed in a very stylish gray suit, shook her head, resting one hand on the doorway. "I knew you shouldn't have gone out driving around town at all hours," she said quietly.

She doesn't know how right she is, Joanna thought drily.

"Now you've caught that terrible flu that everyone is getting."

"No, I don't think so, Mom. I think I'm just exhausted. One day in bed, and I'll be okay."

I'll *never* be okay, she thought glumly.

I'll never get that hideous, decaying face out of my mind.

"Well, if you don't have the flu, I really think you should make an effort to come to church," her mother said, adjusting the string tie that hung down the front of her pleated silk blouse. "Everyone will be asking about you. I received such nice compliments about you at the fund-raiser last night."

Like I'm a prized pedigree dog, Joanna thought bitterly. My, what fine lines she has, Mrs. Collier. Could you put her through her paces for us? Make her heel or sit up and beg?

"I really can't go to church. I'm just going to sleep all day. I'm sorry."

Her mother looked more disappointed than concerned. "You know I won't be back till late tonight? There's a luncheon at the Wilkersons'. And then I have that cocktail party and dinner at the Smiths'."

Well, that's good news, Joanna thought. So go. Please — go, go, go, already.

"Is there anything I can get you, dear? You *do* look very washed out."

Thanks, Mom. Be sure to get that little dig in before you go.

"No, thanks. If there's anything I need, I'll call downstairs for Helen."

"Oh, no. I gave Helen the morning off. She went to visit her sister for a couple of hours. I guess I shouldn't have, but I didn't know. . . ."

That's even better, Joanna thought, burying her head deeper into the pillow. I'll have the whole house to myself. "Go, Mom. You'll be late for church. Please give my regrets to everyone." She rolled onto her side, her back to the door. Maybe her mother would take the hint and leave.

A few minutes later, she heard her mother going

down the carpeted stairs. A few minutes after that, she heard a car door slam and her mother's car start up and then drive off.

Now what?

Lie here all day and think about how my life has turned into a horror show?

Go back to sleep?

I can't sleep *forever* — can I?

What should I do? Pretend that last night didn't happen? Pretend that Dex hasn't become some kind of ghastly creature?

Joanna rolled over, unable to find a comfortable position. She suddenly realized that being all alone wasn't exactly the best idea in the world.

Because all alone there was nothing to take her mind off what had happened.

And she would lie there and see his distorted, leering face with its green, crumbling skin, its patches of protruding skull, its missing front teeth, again and again and again.

"No!"

She sat up and dropped her feet to the carpet.

She started to stand up, but her ankle still hurt from when she had fallen on it, running away from him. She stepped down on it gingerly, then applied more weight. It wasn't so bad, she decided.

Had she really run in terror from Dex? Someone she had once thought she cared about, someone she thought she knew better than she knew anyone else?

Yes. She had leaped off the stoop, dodging away

from his sickening embrace, and had run through the tall weeds of the front yard.

It didn't seem real now. It seemed like a scene she had seen in one of those disgusting horror movies on cable late at night.

But the faint, throbbing pain in her ankle told her it was real.

And the grinning green face she saw again and again in her mind told her it was real.

Last night, when she had run from him and tripped over the tire in the middle of his yard and fallen into the wet weeds, she looked back up to the stoop. Dex, she saw to her relief, wasn't coming after her. In fact, he hadn't moved. He stood stiff-legged, his back to the screen door, staring after her, the hideous grin frozen on his decaying face.

That smell.

Oh, that smell.

Her ankle throbbing with pain, Joanna had hobbled the rest of the way to the car. As soon as she got home, she tore off her clothes, tossed them down the laundry chute, then jumped into the shower.

She took the longest shower of her life, making the water hotter and hotter, trying to wash away that awful smell, trying to wash away the sight of Dex, trying to wash away her fear, her confusion.

But the shower wasn't the answer. Stepping out, she felt as chilled — and as scared — as she had standing on that dimly lit stoop, staring into his unblinking red eyes.

Now it was Sunday morning and the horror of

the scene clung to Joanna like a cold, damp fog.

I should've gone to church with my mother.

No. I've got to talk with someone.

I have to tell someone.

But who?

Mary.

Yes. Mary. Of course. Mary.

When it came right down to it, Mary was her only friend. The only one who knew Dex. Who knew all that happened. Or almost all.

Mary was the only one who would understand. The only one who would believe her.

If *anyone* would believe it.

Joanna wasn't sure she believed it herself.

She walked across the room, stretching, walking gingerly on her bad ankle, and picked up the cellular phone from its holder on her desk. She dialed Mary's number and carried the phone back to the bed, sitting on the edge, staring out the window at what appeared to be a gray, threatening morning.

Someone picked up on the sixth ring. "Hello, Mary?"

"Hi," said a sleep-clogged voice, sounding confused.

"Mary, it's me. Joanna. Did I wake you?"

"No, I had to get up to answer the phone."

"Funny line," Joanna said.

"I stole it from some TV show, I think. What time is it, anyway, Joanna? It's still the middle of the night, isn't it?"

"No. It's nearly nine. Can you come over?"

"What?"

"I really need to talk to you, Mary." Joanna was a little embarrassed by the neediness in her voice. She didn't like sounding like a helpless little girl, which she knew was how she sounded.

But for the first time in her life she really did feel helpless. For the first time in her life she really felt that things were out of control, that she was in a situation she couldn't handle.

It was a strange feeling. She hated it. She wished she sounded more together. She didn't like being so honest, so vulnerable, even with such a close friend. *Especially* with such a close friend.

"So can you come?"

"When? Now?" Mary still sounded half asleep.

"Yeah. Can you?"

"Can't we just talk over the phone, Joanna? I'd like to come, but I'm supposed to go over to my cousin's for lunch, and — "

"I really need you, Mary." This was so embarrassing! Why was Mary giving her a hard time, making it so much more difficult for her? "Something very scary happened last night."

"Okay. I'll be there. Give me an hour or so, okay?"

"Oh, good. Thanks."

"Joanna?"

"Yeah?"

"Are you okay?"

"I — I guess. Yeah. No. I don't know. I'm all mixed up." She could feel herself start to crumble.

She had the feeling she might cry, something she hadn't done in years and years.

So don't start now, she told herself, using all of her strength to hold herself together. Don't start now.

What is there to cry about, anyway?

Just because Dex has joined the Living Dead?

Just because your boyfriend smells like rotting meat and his face is falling off?

Well, he isn't your boyfriend. You don't even care about him. And that's the truth.

You don't care if he lives or . . .

. . . dies?

"See you soon," she said into the phone, then walked over to the desk to put it back.

The sound at the window made her nearly jump out of her skin.

That scrabbling sound.

Someone tapping at the window.

Dex!

No. No — please!

She grabbed the top of the desk for support. Her knees felt weak, about to collapse. The room began to spin.

She was afraid to turn around.

Why was he climbing into her window in daylight? What was he doing here?

"Go away! Please — go away!" she screamed.

Chapter 17

The tapping again.

It wasn't Dex.

Too light to be Dex. Dex would be pounding on the glass, demanding that she open up.

She saw his green face in her mind, that gruesome smile, the dark pit that was his mouth, the glowing red eyes.

Still holding onto the desk, she turned to face the window. A pigeon stood on the outer windowsill. It pecked at the glass. *Tap tap tap*.

Joanna, get a hold of yourself, she warned herself. You can't let yourself go mental because a stupid pigeon taps on the window.

Another shower maybe?

The hot water might make her feel better, help to cleanse away the memories, the pictures, the horrors of the night before that stuck to her skin like stale perspiration.

She took a long, hot shower and shampooed her hair.

Drying herself off, she felt refreshed. A little better.

She got dressed quickly, pulling on a pair of soft, green corduroy slacks and a long-sleeved yellow cotton T-shirt. Then she went downstairs and fixed a breakfast of orange juice, cornflakes, and buttered toast.

She was dropping the breakfast dishes into the dishwasher when Mary's little Toyota pulled into the drive. Joanna dried her hands hurriedly on a dish towel and ran through the front hall to let her friend in.

"Coffee!" Mary roared as soon as Joanna pulled open the door. "Make us coffee! I need a jump start this morning."

"You do look a little out of it," Joanna said, examining Mary's pale face. "Late night last night?"

"No. Nothing special," Mary sighed. She followed Joanna into the kitchen. "Are you feeling better? You sounded so awful over the phone."

"I guess," Joanna said, filling the Krups coffee maker with water.

"You — you sounded so scared, Joanna. Not like yourself at all." Mary pulled off her down vest and tossed it over one of the tall kitchen stools. She climbed up onto the stool next to it and leaned on the white Formica counter, watching Joanna measure out the coffee.

"I — I really don't know where to begin," Joanna said, hating this feeling of vulnerability that was so new to her, but eager to share everything with Mary. "It's about Dex."

"Are you still going out with him?" Mary stifled a yawn with her hand.

Joanna pushed the button on the coffee machine. "Yeah, I guess. I — "

"Him and that other guy. Shep."

"Yeah. Well, I'm going to break up with Dex. For good," Joanna said uncomfortably, sensing Mary's disapproval.

This wasn't the way Joanna wanted this to go. She wanted sympathy from Mary — not disapproval. She wanted some understanding. An explanation, maybe.

An explanation?

Who was she trying to kid?

How could there be an explanation?

"Listen, Mary, something weird is happening to Dex."

"Huh?" That seemed to wake Mary up. She sat up straight on the backless kitchen stool.

"I mean, I think Dex is sick or something."

"Oh. You mean like the flu?"

"No. Not like the flu. Some other kind of disease. Something really serious, I think."

"Joanna — how do you know? Did he tell you he's sick?"

"No. He didn't tell me. But — wait. Let me pour the coffee. Then I'll tell you everything." She reached in the cupboard for the coffee mugs. "It was really nice of you to drive all the way over here so fast. Sorry I woke you."

"That's okay," Mary said. "You sounded so . . . troubled."

Joanna poured the coffee. They added milk and sugar and carried the mugs into the den. Then, sitting beside Mary on the long, red leather couch, Joanna told her the whole story, starting with the date at the dance club, climaxing with the scene of horror on Dex's stoop the night before.

Mary listened in silence, taking long sips of her coffee. Her face remained expressionless. Joanna couldn't tell what she was thinking.

"And that's it," Joanna said. "Up to now, anyway. I just don't know what to think, Mary."

"I don't, either. I really don't," Mary said, staring down at her coffee mug thoughtfully. "You're right, I guess. Dex must have some kind of weird disease. Something that's making his body fall apart."

"But what could it be?" Joanna asked. "I've never seen anyone get a disease like that — not even on *General Hospital*."

It was meant as a joke, but Mary didn't laugh. She seemed to be thinking very hard about something. "The puzzling part is Pete," she said finally. "Pete says that Dex is dead."

"Yeah. When I told him Dex wasn't dead, he looked at me like I had totally lost it," Joanna said. "Pete says he went to his funeral. He still can't talk about the whole thing. He had tears in his eyes last night, Mary."

"This is all so weird," Mary said. "But there's a logical explanation for this. I know we'll figure it out if we keep at it." She held up her coffee mug. "Can I have another cup?"

"Sure. Help yourself," Joanna said. "I want to — "

The phone rang, interrupting her.

She reached over the hump of the couch arm and picked up the phone off the side table. "Hello?"

"Hello, Joanna. Man, I'm glad you're there." The boy's voice was frightened, breathless.

"Who is this?" Joanna cried.

"It's Pete. Joanna — you've got to listen to me."

"What? What's the matter, Pete? You sound so weird."

"Please — don't talk. Just listen. There isn't much time."

"Pete, please — what on earth are you talking about?" A feeling of dread was forming in her chest. She gripped the phone tightly, so tightly her hand started to ache.

"Joanna, I saw him, too."

"Dex?"

"Yes. I saw him." Pete's voice was trembling. It was hard to understand him.

"Pete, try to calm down," Joanna said. "I *told* you I've been seeing Dex. He — "

"Joanna — *please!*" He was shouting now. "You don't understand. Dex is back. Back from the dead!"

"What?!"

"It's true, Joanna. I'm so sorry, but it's true."

"Pete — you're not making any sense. Where are you?"

"Never mind. Just listen to me. He was dead. Dex was really dead. I did go to his funeral. I saw his corpse. But he's come back from the grave, Joanna. He told me."

"He told you?"

"He told me. Oh, lord, he looks so horrible. He's

falling apart. I mean, really. Pieces of him are just falling off. And he smells so bad. He's rotting. Just rotting."

Joanna smelled that ghastly odor once again. Two long showers and she couldn't get rid of that odor. She pictured Dex's grinning, toothless face.

"Pete, listen — "

"*You* listen. Just listen," Pete continued, sounding even more frantic. Joanna could hear traffic noise in the background, a horn honking. Pete was obviously outside in a phone booth somewhere.

"He's come back to punish you, Joanna," he said, his voice trembling. "He's come back from the grave because he wants to pay you back — pay you back for letting him die."

"But I — "

"He knows, Joanna. He knows you ran away and left him. And he's come back to get revenge."

"Pete, stop — I — " Joanna's words choked in her throat. She suddenly felt terribly sick.

"You've got to run!" Pete cried, shouting over a passing bus. "You've got to get out of there. Dex is on his way to your house — now! He's going to kill you, Joanna. He told me. He came back to kill you. He'll be there any moment!"

"Pete — "

She could hear the traffic in the background, but Pete didn't answer.

"Pete?"

The line went dead. The hum of the dial tone returned.

"What was *that* all about?" Mary asked, returning from the kitchen with a fresh cup of coffee.

"Dex. He — "

Joanna stopped and listened.

Yes. She had heard correctly.

There was a loud pounding on the front door.

Chapter 18

"Why do you look so frightened?" Mary asked, putting her coffee cup down on the counter. "It's only someone at the front door."

The knocking repeated, a little louder, a little longer. The doorbell chimed.

"Are you okay?" Mary asked. "I'll get the door."

"No — Mary — " Joanna tried to stop her, but the words caught in her throat. Her heart thudding, she followed Mary into the front hall. "No! Don't!"

But she was too late.

Mary had already opened the door.

Shep walked in, shivering from the cold under his oversized wool overcoat. "Hi, I'm Shep," he said, reaching out to shake Mary's hand.

Mary introduced herself. Shep looked beyond her to Joanna, who was leaning against the wall, breathing a sigh of relief.

"Thank goodness. It's only you," Joanna said breathlessly.

Shep laughed. "What's that supposed to mean? Is that a compliment?"

"We have to go," Joanna said, unable to keep the fear out of her voice.

"Where are you going?" Shep asked, unbuttoning the heavy coat. "I just got here."

"Joanna — what's wrong?" Mary asked. "You look so frightened. Was it that call?"

"Yes. I — " She looked at Shep. He didn't know anything about Dex. He only knew that she had broken up with someone after her car accident so that she could go with him.

How could she begin to tell him what was happening? Especially since she could barely believe it herself.

"You'll think I'm crazy," she said, her heart still pounding in her chest.

"I already think you're crazy," Shep joked, flashing her a warm, reassuring smile. "Hey — do I smell coffee?"

"Yes. I just made a fresh pot," Mary said.

"I'd kill for a cup," Shep said, rubbing his hands together to warm them. "It's freezing out there."

"We don't have time for coffee," Joanna said impatiently. "Dex — he's on his way here."

Shep's handsome face filled with confusion. "Dex?"

"He's coming here?" Mary asked, startled.

"That was Pete on the phone. He — he saw Dex. He knows Dex is back. He — "

"Who's Dex?" Shep asked, draping his coat over

the banister. "What do you mean he's back?"

"It's too long a story," Joanna said, closing her eyes, wishing she could just disappear. "And you wouldn't believe it, anyway."

"Try me," Shep said, walking past her into the kitchen. He sniffed the warm aroma from the coffee maker. "Where are the coffee mugs?"

"Shep — you're not taking me seriously!" Joanna screamed.

Mary and Shep both stared at her, alarmed.

"Joanna — " Mary started.

"He's coming to kill me!" Joanna screamed. "Pete said Dex is coming to kill me!" She knew she sounded hysterical, but she didn't care. Somehow she had to get it across to her two friends that this was an urgent situation, that all three of them were in danger.

"But, Joanna, why?" Mary asked, walking over and putting a hand gently on Joanna's shoulder. "Try to calm down. What did Pete say to make you so — so frightened?"

Joanna pulled angrily away from Mary. "Dex has come back from the grave!" she screamed, feeling her face grow hot. "He told Pete. He's come back from the grave — to kill me!"

Shep stepped back from the coffee maker. He looked over to Mary, as if to say, What's wrong with Joanna?

"I'm not crazy!" Joanna shrieked. "Dex was dead. Pete went to his funeral. But now he's back. Do you understand? He's back! He came back to kill me!"

"Maybe we should get a doctor," Shep said, talking to Mary. "Is Joanna's mother home? Is anyone else in the house?"

"No. No one's home," Mary said. She turned to Joanna. "Listen, why don't we all go over to my house?"

"You don't believe me — do you?" Joanna cried, squeezing her hands into tight fists, so tight her nails dug into her skin.

"We believe you're very upset about something," Shep said softly, slowly. "Why don't we go into the den and sit down? Maybe if we discussed it — "

"There's nothing to discuss," Joanna replied angrily. "Dex is dead. He's on his way. He's going to kill me. He could kill us all."

"Okay. Then let's get out of here," Mary said, looking at Shep. "Get your coat, Joanna. We'll go to my house. Dex will never find you there."

"I don't understand," Shep said. "Is Dex the guy you used to date?"

"Yes," Mary said, pushing Shep toward the front hall. "Joanna can explain it all in the car."

"Explain about a guy who's come back from the grave?"

"You don't believe me! Well, I don't care if you believe me or not!" Joanna cried. "I'm getting out of here." She started toward the front hall, but Shep grabbed her arm and pulled her back.

"I believe you," he said. But he didn't sound very convincing. "But I think we should sit down for a moment, have a cup of coffee, and discuss — "

Before he could finish his sentence, the front door burst open, banging loudly against the wall, making all three of them jump and cry out.

"Shep — you didn't close the door?" Joanna cried.

"I — I thought the maid would," Shep said, looking frightened.

The storm door slammed.

They heard footsteps in the hall.

Dex, walking fast, his eyes wide, stepped stiff-legged into the kitchen.

"Dex — stop!" Pete came running in behind him, his cheeks bright red, breathing hard, his face filled with terror. "Stop! Can you hear me?"

All three of them gasped as Dex staggered under the bright kitchen lights. It was hard to believe that it was Dex. He looked like a creature from a horror movie. A large patch of gray skull protruded through a square bald spot in his hair. All of his teeth were gone. Purple liquid dripped from his eyes. His skin was as green as grass and seemed to be peeling off his cheeks and forehead.

He glared at Joanna, his mouth opened wide in a toothless grin. He staggered forward. It seemed to take every ounce of his strength for him to move. One arm hung limp at his side.

"Dex — stop!" Pete screamed. He turned to Joanna. "I tried to stop him. Really — I tried. But he won't listen to me. I don't think he hears me!"

"Dex — " Joanna tried to cry out to him, but her words choked in her throat. She suddenly felt as if she couldn't breathe, couldn't move.

I'm paralyzed with fear, she thought. So this is what it feels like.

He's going to kill me. I know he's going to kill me. And I'm just going to stand here and let him.

"Joanna, I'm back," Dex said suddenly. His voice could barely be heard. It was a rasping whisper, like wind blowing through the crack in a window.

"Joanna, I'm back. I came back from the grave."

"No! Dex — no!" Joanna managed to find her voice and scream.

"You shouldn't have left me to die, Joanna."

Dex raised his good arm high in front of him. In his hand he held a large, black-handled kitchen knife.

Chapter 19

"Stop him! We've got to stop him!" Pete cried.

He leaped at Dex, reaching for Dex's broad shoulders.

With startling quickness, Dex spun away from Pete. Pete slammed hard into the kitchen counter, looking dazed.

Dex, his dripping eyes staring into Joanna's, staggered forward. "I'm back," he said in his raspy whisper. "Joanna, I'm back."

With one quick chop of his open hand, Shep knocked the big knife from Dex's hand.

"Hey!" Dex cried out in surprise.

He dived for the knife but Joanna got there first.

She didn't even think about it. She grabbed up the knife by the black handle, leaped at Dex, and plunged the blade deep into Dex's chest.

Bright red blood spurted out from Dex's sweatshirt.

His eyes opened wide, first with surprise, then

with terror. He stared at the knife. Then his eyes slowly went up to Joanna.

"No. This isn't right," he said, grimacing in pain.

He slumped to the linoleum and lay in a puddle of his own bright blood.

"No!" Pete screamed, grabbing Joanna and pulling her back, pulling her hard, angrily.

Joanna stared down at Dex's unmoving body. She felt numb. No feeling at all. Then bewilderment as Pete jerked her away.

Mary stood back by the sink, her hands up to her face. Shep leaned against the kitchen counter, looking very frightened and confused.

"What have you done?" Pete cried. "You killed him, Joanna. You killed him!"

"I — what?"

What was Pete saying?

What did he mean?

How could she have killed someone who was already dead?

Pete dropped down to the floor and bent over the body. He put a hand on Dex's neck. Then he placed the back of his hand under Dex's nose.

"Dead," he said, after a long wait. "He's dead."

"Now, wait a minute — " Joanna started. "What's going on here? What do you mean — ?"

"It was just a joke," Pete said softly, looking up at her, still on his knees on the bloodstained floor.

"What?" Shep came up behind Joanna and put his hands on her shoulders.

Joanna leaned back against him, grateful for his support, for his caring.

"Pete — what are you saying?" Mary asked. She had tears running down her cheeks. She was shaking all over. Her eyes kept going down to the still body on the floor.

"It was just a joke," Pete repeated. He rubbed his fingers over Dex's face and held them up to Joanna. His fingers were green. "Just stage makeup," he said.

Joanna swallowed hard. "You mean — ?"

"It was all stage makeup. The green color, the blacked-out teeth, the stuff dripping from his eyes. Him staggering around like Frankenstein's monster. It was all a gag, Joanna."

"Pete — you said you went to his funeral," Joanna said, beginning to realize what really had happened, the horror of what she had just done starting to sink in.

"Just a joke," Pete repeated sadly. "Dex and I cooked it up. To pay you back. To teach you a little lesson. That's all."

"But — "

"But now you've killed him," Pete said, his expression hardening. "Now you've really killed him."

Chapter 20

"Call an ambulance," Shep said, still holding on tightly, comfortingly to Joanna's shoulders. "Maybe he — "

"He's dead," Pete said, sweeping a large hand back nervously through his spiky, blond hair. "It's too late for an ambulance."

"I — I'm going to be sick," Mary said, looking ashen. She ran out of the kitchen, holding her hand over her mouth.

"How could you just kill him like that?" Pete asked Joanna, sounding more accusing than questioning.

"But, Pete — " Joanna didn't know what to say.

"You saw the way Dex came at her with the knife," Shep said, coming to her defense. "She had to react — didn't she? She had to protect herself."

"That's right. It was self-defense," Joanna agreed quickly. Self-defense. Of course.

Self-defense.

Shep, you're a genius.

"I had to protect myself," she repeated. "He came at me . . . and I just reacted." She was starting to breathe normally, starting to feel a little more like herself.

"What a horrible joke," Shep said, looking down at Dex's body. "You know, Pete, you're as much to blame as Joanna."

"I didn't stab him with a knife," Pete said.

"But if you hadn't cooked up this whole thing, if the two of you hadn't planned for Dex to — to — "

"Why, Pete?" Joanna interrupted. "Why pull such a stupid joke?"

"I knew it was stupid," Pete said, sighing. He dropped onto one of the kitchen stools, his shoulders drooping, all of the energy seeming to drain from his body. "I told Dex it was really dumb. But it was that day in the hospital, Joanna. That day I came to tell you that Dex was dead. That's as far as we were going to take the joke. But then — "

"But then what?" Joanna demanded, anger replacing her fear.

"Then when you didn't even cry, when you didn't even look that upset, Dex decided to take the joke as far as he could."

"And you and he did the whole thing just to frighten me?" Joanna asked.

"You deserved it — the way you treated Dex. You used him." Pete's voice softened. "Dex loved acting. And he loved makeup. You should've seen him after he got out of the hospital. He was so turned on by the whole idea. He spent days just getting the right smell to make him smell like he was decaying."

"Ugh." Joanna made a face, remembering that sour smell.

"It was all just a stupid joke that went too far," Pete said sadly, shaking his head. "You're right, Joanna. I'm as much at fault as you are."

"But what are we doing to *do*?" Joanna demanded. "We can't just stand around here talking about it."

"We've got to call the police," Shep said, squeezing Joanna's shoulder.

She stepped away from him and started to pace back and forth. "We can't," she said, thinking hard. "Do you really think the police would believe this story? They'll just think that I killed him."

"But we're all witnesses. We saw what happened," Shep said.

"They won't believe any of us. They'll think we made up the story after Dex was killed," Joanna said.

Mary came back into the kitchen, still looking pale and shaky. "Joanna's right," she said, sitting down on one of the tall stools, holding on to the counter edge. "The police will never believe the true story. We've got to get rid of the body. Drag it out to the woods or something."

"Yes!" Joanna cried. She felt like hugging Mary. What an excellent idea! "Mary's right. There's nothing we can do for Dex now. Why should our lives all be ruined because of a stupid joke?"

Joanna realized she was breathing normally again. Her heart had gone back to its normal beat. She was starting to feel a lot stronger, a lot more in control.

"Yes, we have to get rid of the body," she repeated.

Shep shook his head. "It's no good," he said. "They'll catch us. Dex's family will know where he was going. They'll — "

"He doesn't have a family," Joanna interrupted. "He only has an old aunt who never knows where he goes. There's no way the police can trace this to us. No way. Especially if we take the body some place far away."

"No. I'm sorry. We have to tell the police. They'll believe the truth if we all just — "

Joanna glared angrily at Shep. "Why are you being such a wimp?" she cried. "You know, *your* life will be ruined by this, too. Are you really willing to give up your entire future because of Dex's stupid joke?"

Shep didn't answer. He walked over to the back door and stared out the window at the long, sweeping backyard.

"Yeah. I guess you're right," Pete said reluctantly, staring hard at Joanna. "There's nothing we can do for Dex now."

Mary turned her head away. Her shoulders were shaking.

"Don't cry, Mary," Joanna said. "We'll be okay — once we get rid of the body." She wanted to go over and comfort her friend. But she was afraid she might start crying, too.

She didn't want to cry. She wanted to keep herself in control.

She wanted to keep thinking clearly, to stay alert.

They were going to get out of this mess.

She wasn't going to let Dex ruin her life.

She never should have gotten involved with him in the first place.

Mary suddenly turned back. "Pete and I will take the body," she said resolutely. She dabbed at her wet cheeks with a tissue.

"I'm not helping," Shep said, still staring out into the backyard. "I won't stop you from doing it. But I don't think it's right. I won't help."

"That's okay," Pete said quickly, standing up and walking over to Dex's body. "Mary and I can get Dex into her trunk. We'll take him to the woods near his house."

"Shep and I will clean up," Joanna said, looking at Shep.

"Yeah. Okay," he agreed, looking very unhappy.

Joanna heard the front door open and close.

Everyone froze.

"Who's that?"

"Your mom?"

"It's Helen," she told them. "The maid. Mom

gave her the morning off. But now she's back. Quick — " She pointed to the body. "Out the back door. Hurry!"

Looking frightened, Pete bent down and grabbed Dex under the shoulders. He started to pull. The body slid across the linoleum. "I think I can drag him," he told Mary. "Just get the door, okay?"

Mary hurried to the kitchen door and held it open for Pete.

"I'll call you later," Joanna said, listening to the maid's footsteps in the hall. "Good luck. I know we're doing the right thing."

Just get it out of the house, she thought.

She breathed a sigh of relief as Pete and Mary disappeared out the door, and the door slammed behind them.

Shep stood, leaning against the kitchen counter, looking very upset.

Helen's footsteps grew louder, then fainter.

She's going to her room to change, Joanna thought. Then she'll come into the kitchen.

She looked down at the puddle of dark blood on the floor.

"Well, they're gone," Shep said quietly. "I hope the neighbors won't see what they're dragging to the car."

"The neighbors can't see. Their houses are too far away," Joanna said, thinking hard. "Besides, there're all the trees."

She went to the drawer and pulled out a small

steak knife. Then she advanced quickly on Shep.

Shep looked up, surprised.

He saw the knife in her hand and, as she strode toward him, a purposeful look on her face, his expression turned to fear.

"Joanna — stop!" Shep cried. "What are you going to do with that?"

Chapter 21

Joanna grabbed Shep's left hand, turned it up, and sliced a long line across the palm with the knife.

Bright red blood seeped to the surface along the line of the cut, then quickly dripped to the floor.

"Joanna — ?"

Shep pulled his hand out of her grip, staring at the flowing blood, then at her, horrified.

"Helen!" Joanna shouted, tossing the knife onto the counter. "Helen!"

"Yes?" the maid called from down the hall.

"Could you come here, please?" Joanna called. "My friend has cut himself. I'm afraid there's a lot of blood on the floor. Could you come clean it up?"

Helen came rushing in, buttoning the sleeves of her white uniform. She was a short, chubby woman, with a round face that frowned in surprise as she saw the large puddle of blood on the floor. She looked over to Shep, who was busily wrapping his bleeding hand in paper towels.

"You should go to a doctor. You've lost a lot of

blood," Helen said, hurrying to the mop closet.

"He'll be okay," Joanna said.

Shep glared at her. He strode past her and into the front hall, heading to the door, holding the towels tightly around his cut hand.

Joanna followed him to the door. "I'm sorry, Shep," she said, whispering so that Helen wouldn't hear. "I had to do something. I didn't want to hurt you. But it was the first thing I — "

"You're cold, Joanna," he said, his hand on the door handle. "You're not really human. I had no idea how cold you were."

He was out the door before she could reply.

She watched him get into his car, back down the drive, and roar away. Then she closed the front door, locked it, and hurried up the stairs to her room.

She sat down on the edge of the still unmade bed.

"I'm going to be okay," she said aloud.

I'm going to be okay.

This is all going to work out fine.

I'm going to be okay.

She repeated the word *okay* over and over until it didn't seem like a real word anymore.

Then she realized that she was trembling all over.

She saw Shep in school on Monday. His hand was bandaged. He walked right past, pretending he didn't see her.

She sighed, feeling sorry for herself.

Shep, I care about you, she thought.

We've got to get back together. We're so right for each other.

She thought of chasing after him, running up behind him, throwing her arms around his broad shoulders. I'll beg him to forgive me, she thought. I'll beg him. I'll apologize a thousand times, throw myself on his mercy.

She stood in the middle of the hall, watching the back of him until he turned a corner and disappeared.

She tried to concentrate on midterm exams, but it was nearly impossible.

Her mind kept wandering back to all that had happened.

Dex's face, his toothless, grinning, green face haunted her thoughts.

She couldn't study. She couldn't think straight.

Monday night she called Mary to find out what had happened with Dex's body. But Mary couldn't talk. Her parents were in the room.

Tuesday she drifted through two exams, struggling to concentrate. Afterwards, she was sure she messed up on both of them.

Wednesday and Thursday went by in a blur of studying and more exams. Thursday night she picked up the phone to call Shep.

But she put it back down.

What if he refused to talk to her? What if he refused to come to the phone?

After school on Friday, she thought of skipping her tennis lesson. But at the last minute, she decided to go ahead with it. A little exercise might do her good:

Maybe it would take her mind off Dex, off the blood-smeared kitchen floor, his body lying so still on the floor. Maybe it would take her mind off losing Shep.

I'll work up a good, honest sweat, she thought. I've got to get my blood flowing again.

Blood.

She had to stop thinking about blood.

"I'm going to be okay," she said, juggling her bookbag and tennis racquet as she passed through the glass doors of the tennis club.

I'm going to be okay. It wasn't my fault. No one will ever know.

Gary was her new instructor. He looked more like a wrestler than a tennis player, with his long, curly black hair, his biceps bulging out of his T-shirt, his broad chest. "Let's warm up a little first," he said, dragging a basket of yellow tennis balls onto the court.

The club was crowded, mostly with kids having their after-school lessons. Voices echoed off the high rafters. Joanna had never noticed how noisy the club was before.

Gary hit some easy ones over the net. Joanna stood in place, hitting them back with her forehand, swinging casually, the racquet light in her hand.

After hitting five or six balls, something made her turn around. She looked back to the spectators' area behind the mesh screen.

That's where Dex had stood, she remembered.

That's where he had stood, looking so green, so weird.

She remembered seeing him in the parking lot afterwards, his eyes glowing red. It was so frightening.

And all so phony.

Just a fake.

She couldn't believe Dex had played such an elaborate prank. All that makeup. All that time and work.

And where had it gotten him?

Into a shallow grave in the woods.

Or maybe no grave at all. Maybe he had just been tossed into some thick bushes or high weeds.

She should've tried Mary again. Or called Pete. She should've found out what had happened with the body.

But somehow it was just as well not knowing.

The body was gone. Dex was gone.

So why was she looking for him now?

"Joanna? Joanna?"

She realized that Gary had been calling to her for some time.

"Are you looking for someone?" he asked.

"No," she said, still distracted.

"Shall we play a game?" He twirled his racquet in his hand.

"No," she said. "I — I've got to go."

She couldn't concentrate. She didn't want to be there.

I can't play on this court, she thought. I keep having the feeling that Dex is standing back there, watching me, staring at me with those frightening red eyes.

"Joanna — ?" Gary called after her.

But she turned and ran to the locker room without looking back.

I've got to get out of here. Out. Out. Out.

I've got to stop thinking about Dex.

What's wrong with me, anyway? I didn't even care that much about Dex. Why can't I get him out of my mind now?

She answered her own question: because you killed him.

She changed quickly into her street clothes. She drove around aimlessly for nearly an hour before heading home.

Maybe if I talk to Mary and hear the end of the story, I'll be able to put it out of my mind, she thought.

The end of the story. Would there *be* an end to the story?

She had read the morning newspaper every day, grabbing it up as soon as she came downstairs, much to her mother's surprise. But there had been no story about anyone finding Dex's body in the woods. She watched the local TV news at six each evening. They didn't have the story, either.

So, maybe the story had already ended.

She just had to talk to Mary. See how Mary was doing. Maybe Mary was doing better than Joanna. Maybe she wasn't thinking about Dex, thinking about the murder every minute of the day.

Maybe Mary can help me get it out of my mind.

But when Joanna got home, her mother was there. She had to talk to her mother, pretend to have a conversation. She talked about her midterms, how hard they were. She talked about her tennis lesson, making up some funny stories about the new instructor who looked like a wrestler.

That made her mother laugh.

Joanna, you're such a good liar, she told herself.

If only you could lie to *yourself*.

She wanted to go upstairs and call Mary, but Mrs. Collier stopped her from leaving the room. "Helen's just about to serve dinner," she said. "She's made your favorite — leg of lamb. I have to go out tonight, but I thought for once we'd have a quiet dinner, just the two of us."

So Joanna had to make up more stories to tell her mother, stories about school, stories about Shep and what a great guy he was.

"You've barely touched your lamb," Mrs. Collier said after a while.

"I — I'm not all that hungry," Joanna said, which was certainly true.

"Are you feeling okay? You look kind of . . . tired." Joanna's mother was constantly accusing her of looking tired.

Joanna looked up from her practically untouched plate at her mother. For a brief moment, she felt as if she might tell her mother what was troubling her.

"You see, I killed Dex, Mom. He was playing a

joke on me, trying to make me think he had come back from the grave, and I stabbed him in the chest with a knife. Then Pete and Mary took his body and hid it in the woods. And that's why I'm having a little trouble digging into this lamb on my plate."

Wouldn't that go over big?

Joanna couldn't believe she had even *for a second* considered telling her mother what had happened.

I must be *really* losing it, she thought.

Helen served apple pie with cinnamon ice cream for dessert. Joanna managed to get a little of it down. Then she excused herself, and gave her mom a quick kiss on the forehead — which startled Mrs. Collier, who wasn't used to much affection from her daughter. "Joanna — ?" she started.

But Joanna was already running up to her room to call Mary.

She sat down at her desk, breathing heavily from running up the stairs. As she reached to pick up the phone, it rang.

Startled, she grabbed it up before the first ring had ended.

"Hello?"

"Hi, Joanna." A boy's voice cut through the static on the line.

"Shep? Is that you?"

Muffled laughter on the other end. "No, Joanna. It's me. Dex. I'm back, Joanna. This time I really *did* come back."

Chapter 22

"See you," Dex's voice said over the static.

"Dex?"

"See you."

Then the line went dead. Joanna uttered a little cry and sat staring at the phone.

She saw Dex's green face again, the skin peeling off. And she saw him lying on her kitchen floor in the puddle of blood.

Real blood.

Really dead.

It had all been real.

And now he was back.

It has to be a joke, she thought, feeling cold all over.

Someone is pretending to be Dex.

But it sounded so much like him. She even recognized the muffled laugh.

But Dex was dead. She'd killed him. Felt the knife go in. Seen the blood.

Oh, help me. Somebody — help me!

I can't think straight!

I've got to figure this out. I've got to know what is happening!

She dialed Mary's number. It rang four times. Finally Mary's mother picked it up.

"Mary can't come to the phone now. She's very busy."

"Oh, please. I've really got to talk to her." Joanna didn't recognize her own voice. It was so pinched with fear, so . . . desperate.

"I'll have her call you back."

Not good enough, Joanna thought. Not fast enough.

I've got to get out of this house, away from here.

"See you," Dex had said. Dead Dex.

"See you."

Did that mean he was on his way over to her house?

Dead Dex was on his way to . . . to do *what*??

Joanna dropped the cellular phone, jumped up, and ran down the stairs, taking them two at a time. "Mom? Mom?"

"She just left," Helen called from the kitchen. "Some club meeting or something."

I've got to get out of here, Joanna thought, her heart thudding.

I'll go to Mary's. She grabbed her coat from the closet and searched the front table for her car keys.

"I'm going over to a friend's," she called to Helen.

Helen called something back, but Joanna was already out the door.

Mary will know what to do, she told herself as the houses whirred by on both sides. It was a clear, cold night. Everything seemed to be in sharp focus, as if she were looking through a very expensive, fine camera lens.

Mary will know what to do.

But that was silly, wasn't it?

Why should Mary know what to do about someone who has come back from the grave?

Dead Dex.

Dead Dex . . . who wouldn't stay dead.

A few minutes later, she pulled the car into Mary's driveway and cut the headlights. The front of the house was dark. The porchlight wasn't on.

Joanna stepped out of the car and waited for her eyes to adjust to the total blackness. After a while, the black outline of the house loomed in front of her, against a somewhat lighter sky. Shrubs and a low, bent tree came into dark focus.

Joanna turned and looked back at the street. There were no streetlights.

She had a sudden chill.

Wrapping her unbuttoned coat around her, she started walking quickly up to the dark house. The ground felt hard and frozen beneath her sneakers. Her breath sent clouds of fog in front of her.

As she neared the front stoop, she could see lights on in the back of the house.

I'm almost there, she thought, nearly tripping over a smooth stone placed at the edge of the flag-stone walk that led to the front door.

Why does it have to be so dark?

She regained her balance and started to jog up to the front stoop.

Mary will know what to do.

I just need to talk with her, that's all.

She raised her hand to knock on the front door, then stopped.

She smelled him first.

That sour smell. That smell of rotting meat. But different from the phony garbage smell. Worse. Raw. Raw and rotting at the same time.

Then she felt the bony tap on her shoulder.

"Ohh."

She spun around, unable to breathe.

"Dex!"

In the darkness, she could see that one of his eyes was gone. There was nothing there but an empty socket.

"Joanna," he said, his voice a harsh whisper. "Why did you kill me?"

Chapter 23

It was so dark.

The smell was overpowering.

Joanna realized she'd been holding her breath. Now she let it out in a loud gasp.

"Why did you kill me, Joanna? Look — I'm still bleeding."

He held up his shirt. The wound was large and dark.

"Dex — I didn't mean — " She looked for an escape route, but he had backed her up against the front door.

She looked away. She couldn't bear to look at the empty eye socket, at his sagging, crumbling skin, at the gaping, dark wound in his chest.

Even in the blackness of the night he looked terrifying.

"Why did you kill me?" he repeated, his voice so weak she could barely hear him, the words floating out over his toothless gums.

"Help! Somebody help!" she screamed at the top

of her voice, and started to run, her sneakers slipping on the hard, wet ground.

"Don't run! It was so hard to come back!" Dex cried.

He was right behind her.

"No! Go away! Go away!"

"I went away, Joanna. But I came back."

He grabbed her shoulder. Then his hand slid down and he tackled her around the waist.

They both tumbled to the cold ground. He landed on top of her and pressed her into the dirt.

"No!" she screamed.

She was about to scream again, but stopped.

"Hey — " she said, pushing him hard, trying to shove him off her. "I can touch you." She grabbed his arm. "You're solid."

He was breathing hard from the short chase.

She reached up and touched his face. She pulled off a chunk of plastic makeup.

"You creep! You're not dead! This is still part of your ghastly joke!"

A broad, toothless smile formed on his face. "You're right," he said in his normal voice. "I'm alive." Then he added, "But the joke is over."

"Get off me! It's cold down here. You're ruining my coat!"

"The joke is over, Joanna."

"Did you hear me? Get off! What do you think you're doing? Ugh. You stink!"

She struggled to climb out from under him, but he was too strong.

"The joke is over," he repeated.

Reaching into his jacket pocket, he pulled out a switchblade knife and flicked open the blade.

"Dex — put that down!" she screamed.

The porch light came on. He looked even more gruesome in the shadowy yellow light.

And he looked angry.

"The knife is real," Dex said, staring down at her, holding the knife in front of her face. "It's real like me."

"Dex — "

"It's not a fake this time. It's not a retractable stage knife."

"Dex — *please!*" Joanna cried. "What do you *want?*"

"I want to show you that this knife is real," he said, bringing it down quickly.

Chapter 24

He plunged the knife blade into the dirt beside her head.

He was only trying to scare her.

"See?" he said, breathing hard. "It's real. A real knife."

With a burst of strength she shoved him off and struggled to her feet. He regained his balance quickly and stood beside her.

"Why, Dex?" she asked, watching the knife in his hand. "Why are you doing this?"

He turned away, and looked up to the front stoop. The porch light had come on, but the door was still closed. When he turned back to her, his face was filled with hatred.

"Why? Because you didn't care about me." He angrily pulled off the phony eye socket.

"But, Dex — "

"I loved you, Joanna." His voice broke on the word *love*. "You were the best thing that ever happened to me. I cared so much about you. And then . . ." He looked down at the knife.

"I cared about you, too," Joanna said. But it didn't sound convincing even to her.

"Then when I fell off that cliff, you didn't care whether I lived or died."

"Is that what Pete told you?" Joanna asked quickly. "Well, that's a lie, Dex. That isn't true. I — "

"It *is* true!" he screamed, his dark eyes burning into hers. "You can't lie to me anymore, Joanna. You didn't care whether I lived or died that night. And when Pete came to see you in the hospital — "

"I was totally drugged in the hospital!" Joanna cried. "I was hurt, *too*, you know. When Pete came to see me — "

"He told you I was dead, and you didn't even react."

"I was drugged. I wasn't myself, Dex. I cried for days."

He laughed, a bitter laugh. "It's no good, Joanna. It's no good. When you stuck that knife in me last Sunday, and I died a second time, you still didn't care."

"I was so upset — "

"You just wanted my body out of the way. That's all you cared about. I was just some mess to clear away. So you and your rich boyfriend wouldn't have your lives disturbed."

"Pete is behind all of this — isn't he?" Joanna asked, looking over to her car.

It was so close, yet so far.

If she could just get into the car and lock the doors. . . .

"This is all Pete's idea, isn't it, Dex?"

He shook his head. He flicked the knife blade in and out nervously, staring hard at her all the while, his breath coming out in small, gray puffs.

"Pete helped me. That's all," he said softly. "Pete helped. But I don't need help now."

"What do you mean? What are you going to do?"

She looked to the house. Why didn't the door open? Why didn't someone come rushing out to save her?

Couldn't they hear all the yelling out here?

He took a step toward her. "I'm not going to die a *third* time," he said, his voice without expression, flat and calm now.

Insanely calm, she thought.

He's crazy. Dex is truly crazy.

"I'm not going to die again," he said. "It's your turn!"

She backed toward the drive.

He raised the knife and lunged at her.

"No!"

He stumbled over the smooth stone at the end of the walk, the same stone Joanna had stumbled over before.

The knife bounced out of his hand and stopped at Joanna's feet. She bent over quickly and picked it up.

"You're wrong, Dex," she said. "It's your turn *again!*"

Chapter 25

"Joanna — stop!"

Mary came running out of the house at full speed, wearing only jean cutoffs and a T-shirt.

Joanna turned toward her, startled, forgetting the knife in her hand. "Mary — what are you — ?"

She expected Mary to stop. But Mary ran right at her, pushing her hard, grabbing the knife out of her hand.

"Get away from him!" Mary screamed angrily.

Surprised by her friend's reaction, Joanna took a step back.

"Were you really going to kill him?" Mary screamed. "Haven't you done enough to him?"

She walked over to Dex and put her arm around him. He bent his head low, and she kissed him on the cheek.

"Mary — !" Joanna suddenly felt weak. The yellow porch light flickered. Shadows seemed to circle her on the dark ground.

This isn't real, she thought.

"Mary — you were in on this, too?" she asked, struggling to get the words out.

Still holding onto Dex, Mary smiled triumphantly. "It was all my idea," she said softly. "Right from the beginning."

"But why, Mary? I thought we were best friends. I thought — " Joanna just stared at them, waiting for the shadows to stop spinning, waiting for the darkness, the incredible heavy darkness to lift. "Why?"

"You had everything," Mary said bitterly, "and what did I have? Nothing. You had the big house, the expensive car — you had Dex. He was the one thing I wanted in the world." She looked up at Dex. He hugged her tight.

"But Mary — "

"It just broke my heart, Joanna. It broke my heart that you had Dex, and you didn't even care about him. You used him. Like you use everybody. It was all a game to you. You told me that yourself. He was a pet, a belonging, just one of the hundreds of things that belong to you."

"You're not being fair," Joanna said, staring hard at the knife, which was still clenched tightly in Mary's hand.

"Oh, yes, I am," Mary said heatedly. "Time and again you told me how Dex meant nothing to you. You were so *awful* to him. Standing him up and then bragging about it to me. Going out with Shep behind his back."

Mary was getting more and more worked up.

Joanna kept staring at the knife, wondering how over the edge Mary was, wondering if she was upset enough to use it.

"It was so ironic," Mary continued, her voice high and tight, her eyes wide with anger. "Because all the time you were telling me how little Dex meant to you, that's all I wanted — just Dex."

Before she realized it, Joanna found herself laughing. "Hey, listen, Mary — you're welcome to him. Really. Be my guest."

She started walking quickly to the car.

"Don't laugh at me, Joanna!"

In a fury, Mary leaped at her, holding the knife high.

"No! Stop!" Joanna turned just in time, and stumbled backwards onto the ground.

Mary raised the knife high, but Dex grabbed her arm.

"Let me kill her! Let me kill her!" Mary screamed.

But Dex gently pulled the knife from her hand and tossed it onto the ground. "Come on," he said softly, holding her close to him. "Easy. Take it easy." She was still breathing hard, but his words seemed to calm her. "Let's go inside. Let's forget all about Joanna. Let's forget this whole crazy time."

She glared at Joanna, then turned her face away.

They walked arm in arm up to the house.

They never looked back.

Joanna picked herself up and watched them until

the door closed behind them and the porch light went off.

Then she picked up the knife. The blade slid easily into the handle.

It was a phony stage prop.

At home in her room, Joanna sat at the desk, holding the knife in her hand, rolling it around between her fingers.

It's as phony as I am, she thought.

Mary was right. About everything.

And now here I am, all alone. I've lost everyone. No one is left.

I don't have a friend, a single friend. Maybe I never did.

Because I never really knew how to care about any of them.

Before she realized it, hot tears were running down her cheeks, and she was sobbing.

It felt so strange.

I haven't cried in years, she thought.

I haven't cried since . . .

She thought hard. When? When?

I haven't cried since the night Daddy left us.

For once, she didn't hold her true feelings back. She let herself cry, the tears flowing down her cheeks. She cried until she was all cried out.

To her surprise, she felt a little better.

She wiped her eyes, then tucked the knife away in a desk drawer.

Then she took a deep breath, picked up the phone, and dialed Shep.

He picked up on the third ring.

"Shep?"

"Hi . . . Joanna."

"Shep, I have to talk to you," she said. "I — I'm back from the grave."

He didn't understand what she meant.

She hoped he'd give her a chance to explain.

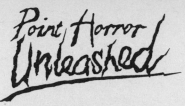

CALLING ALL POINT HORROR FANS!

Welcome to the new wave of fear. If you were
scared before, you'll be *terrified* now...

At Gehenna's Door
Peter Beere

Transformer
Philip Gross

The Carver
Jenny Jones

House of Bones
Graham Masterton

Darker
Andrew Matthews

Blood Sinister
The Vanished
Celia Rees

The Hanging Tree
Paul Stewart

Catchman
Chris Wooding

Look out for:
The Ghost Wife
Susan Price

Point Horror Unleashed.
It's one step beyond...